THE DESTINY OF MARY

THE DESTINY OF MARY

by

MICHELLE MYERS

Design by: Vince Pannullo
Print by: RJ Communication.

Printed in the United States of America

ISBN: 978-0-578-09667-4

CONTENTS

DEDICATION

This book is dedicated to all the remarkable Marys of this world, my Flower of Judah, Thunder of Praise, Sword of Justice and my precious little Lightening of God.

And for my dear Chase:
We must stop judging books by their covers, and realize the most amazing
Qualities aren't always seen on the outside.

ACKNOWLEDGEMENT

I would like to thank the Lord Jesus for being born in the flesh. Thank you, Lord for my life and all the loving people that you have placed in it. To my mother, Grace, thank you for allowing me to listen to the Lord, and teaching me to be honest. To my children, Destiny, Diamond, RonDavid, Rose, Tyler, Tyson, Angel Baby Sarah, and Sunshine, thank you for allowing mommy the time to type, edit and work for Yeshua. I love you so much, and can only pray that you will do amazing things as you step into your destiny for Christ. To my brother, Chris, thank you for teaching me the true meaning of faith. To Cami, my sister and friend, thank you for all your hard work and for embracing the craziness! To all my family at Freedom Encounter Ministries, may the Lord bless you and keep you for your faithfulness to Him. To my niece Ali Persinger, I can't wait to see how God uses you to light the world on fire. To everyone at Michelle 25, Key of Heaven Productions and Blue Sand Ministries, thank you! To all those who advised, helped, suggested or simply prayed for me...thank you. Isaiah 22:22

INTRODUCTION

AS I stood looking at the most beautiful creature I had ever seen, the words coming from his mouth sounded impossible. How could it be me that our Lord had chosen me? My feet felt like they had been dipped in fire or something, and I didn't exactly feel sick, but the nausea overwhelming me was real.

The angel told me not to be afraid. I had jumped about a foot off the ground when he first appeared; but his voice...his voice was so calming and quiet. It melted on me like tiny raindrops of truth, and I loved every drop.

Ancient instinct made me place my hands on my stomach. If what he was saying was true, and every part of me knew it was, the Promised one, the seed of God would grow within me. He was speaking my destiny...The Destiny of Me...Mary.

CHAPTER ONE

JUST A GIRL

"MARY," my mother shouted from the entrance to the room.

"Yes," I answered, quickly throwing off the covers of my bed.

"Rebecca is waiting for you."

I laughed. "Rebecca is waiting for me? I think I'm the one that has been waiting."

"Well, be that as it may, she's here now. Are you two going straight to school afterward?"

"Yeah, probably. I don't think we'll have time to do much else. Hey, do you know where my blue shirt is?"

My mother walked over to my closet and produced the shirt. "Here, and don't forget we have to take Colin to his math lessons and Amber to dance class."

"I will," I promised from the bathroom as I dried my face and put my toothbrush up.

I had been so excited about getting our science project done, and Rebecca had blown me off for the past two days. Her cousin from Italy had been visiting for the past week, and while I could understand the preoccupation, we only had a few more days to get done.

I rushed down the steps toward the kitchen. There was my

best friend, scarfing down one of my mother's famous blueberry muffins.

"Hey, Becs, what's with the early wake up call?" I asked as she stood to hug me.

She swallowed. "I just figured you were on the verge of wanting to strangle me for ditching you so much. I thought we could head out to the lake and check the seedlings, and then go to school, if that's cool."

"Yeah, of course," I responded and grabbed a muffin. "Did your mom let you use her car?"

"Uh, huh," she answered wiping her mouth. "She said it was fine as long as I was back in time after school to take her to work."

My mother cleared her throat. "Yes, Mary, don't forget to be back right after school. I don't want to leave you here by yourself tonight. There are too many new faces in the neighborhood for me. I'd feel more comfortable if you tagged along and did your work at Amber's dance class. And don't forget, Joseph will be here to fix the roof. It would be too loud for you to concentrate anyway."

"I know mom." Grabbing my jacket off the post, I stopped to give her a kiss. "I'll be here right after school."

Rebecca and I headed out the door to her mom's car. It wasn't the prettiest thing in the world, but it saved us having to walk or take the bus. The walking part I didn't mind, but riding the bus was a whole other ordeal.

I was never one to crave popularity or be in some certain crowd. If anything, I got pegged as one of the religious freaks at school. Everyone knew that my family was one of the families that believed in the prophecy. It wasn't that I was ashamed, but the confrontations about it were downright crazy sometimes.

The bus was a metal cage of captivity, upon which you had to undergo persecution at the hands of the inmates. I'd seen a couple of the brave souls get pounded later for talking about a new leader coming to rule.

Most people left me alone. I stayed to myself and tried to be as invisible as possible. When conversation about the prophecy would arise, I would just act as if I had my Ipod too loud, but I always heard them.

I didn't have my license yet; only fifteen, I hadn't even thought about getting my permit or signed up for driver's education. Rebecca was a year older than me, but in the same grade, so she drove us when she could. My family only had one old car, which my dad somehow drove every day to work at the mill. On days that Rebecca's mom worked the evening shift, we always used her car to get to school.

The wind was crisp as it wrapped around my face, but I knew the rays of the sun would soon blanket us with warmth.

"You want the radio on or off?' Rebecca asked as she started the car.

"Off is fine with me," I answered and shut the door. "Hey, so how's stuff with your cousin going?"

She laughed. "Fine, I guess. I can hardly understand half of what he's saying. My mom said he knows about as much English as a two year old."

"I thought he'd been here before."

"He has, but it was when he was five. And that visit was only for a few days or something. Anyway, did you bring the logbook?'

I reached in my backpack. "Of course, oh, and I redid the graph."

"Mary, do you always have to be so perfect about everything?"

Shaking my head I mocked being astonished. "Why do you always say that? You know, according to the law, the Creator commanded that we do all things as unto Him. I'm just trying to follow along best I can."

The only sound for a moment was the engine of the car. I knew I'd mentioned a hard subject with Rebecca.

"Sorry, Becs, I wasn't trying to bring up stuff about Adam."

She looked over at me with a weak smile. "I know, Mary... it's all good."

Adam was Rebecca's older brother. Three years ago he had taken off for the university, so full of promise and life. He had been a staunch advocate of free speech and standing up for what you believe. The prophecy of the new leader coming to help the less fortunate and spread justice in the land was something that gave Adam such a drive.

We knew many families that believed, but the military wasn't fond of the fanatics spreading rumors and words about a new leader. Adam never paid much attention to the soldiers, and as a teenager got in trouble many times for talking about the prophecy.

After six months at the university, some students staged a protest about some unfair things in the government. Adam was determined to help set the injustice of the world right, and had little regard for what he called 'false authority.' A few days after the protest, he was found dead behind some buildings on campus. The police said it was an unsolved homicide, but we believers all knew what had happened. Adam was another in a long line of us to be silenced for speaking against the law.

Ever since then, Rebecca had a really hard time dealing with any kind of reference toward the Creator. And even though I knew she still believed, she was upset and felt like she'd been betrayed when Adam died. I sympathized with her, but couldn't believe that the Creator had failed us. I knew one day someone would come to make the wrongs of our world right. I had to believe.

We got out the car and headed over to the garden. My cheeks were cold, but it was still nice to be outdoors. It didn't matter much to me what the temperature was, as long as I was outside, I was happy.

"It feels awesome out here," I said and smiled at her.

"Yeah," she agreed. "Hey, hand me the log so I can write down the measurements. Did you bring your tape measure?"

I held it up for her to see. "Yes, ma'am, I sure did." Handing her the log, I knelt down. "The ground seems so wet here. Did it rain last night?"

She shrugged. "Maybe, either that or there's some sort of pipe issue."

I looked up at her and laughed. "Pipe issue?"

"Yeah. There are pipes that run from the water to a couple of houses around here. Didn't you know this was a spring?"

Shaking my head I reached over and measured our first plant. "Nope. I thought all this time it was just a lake. This one is four inches."

"Really?" She asked. "Just last week plant number one was only about three inches."

"Well, I don't know what happened, but between this extra moisture and extra growth, maybe someone dumped some miracle water on our little experiment."

Just then behind us a loud noise made me jump. I stood to my feet having dropped the tape measure.

"What was that?" I asked walking closer to her.

Before she had time to answer, Rebecca and I found ourselves being confronted by two men in military uniforms. My heart beat so loud it made my ears hurt. What in the world were they doing here?

"Hello, ladies," the tallest one said.

We stood silent not quite sure what to answer.

"You girls out for a morning stroll?" He walked right up to us and I felt Rebecca start to shake.

I swallowed hard. "We're just checking on our experiment," I sputtered out, trying to make the tenor of my voice confident.

The other guy sort of laughed, but it wasn't a happy noise. It made my insides crawl with disgust.

"Well," he continued. "What kind of experiment; something we could help you with?"

Shaking my head I took a small step in front of Rebecca. "No, sir, but thank you. We were actually done and need to get to school."

Jerking Rebecca's arm, I pulled her backward and bent down to retrieve my tape measure. She didn't seem to know how to function, and the alarm in her eyes sent chills up my spine.

I noticed that the other man had moved over a little, and wasn't directly in front of us. I felt tense, but a flame started somewhere deep inside of me and I was more mad than afraid.

"What's your hurry?" The other guy asked.

Standing up, I took Rebecca's hand again and led her to start walking.

"Like I said," I answered him coldly. "We need to get to school."

Rebecca stumbled on something and my arm jerked as she

fell to the ground. Before I could respond, the first guy that had been talking reached over to grab her. I knew the scream that left her was completely involuntary. It echoed throughout the trees, and it was as if everything moved in slow motion.

I glanced over to the man's startled face, but my attention was drawn to a flock of birds above that seemed to be pulled by invisible strings. To this day I couldn't tell you how long it was, but it seemed like forever minus a moment...the moment I looked into my friends face and saw terror like I had never seen before.

"Don't touch her!" I yelled, grabbing onto his arm.

Suddenly strong arms were behind me, holding me around my waist. "Calm down, little girl," I heard the other man's voice. "Nobody is going to do anything to you."

There isn't an explanation for what happened next. As loud as I've ever heard it, someone called my name. "Mary!" A voice shattered through my nightmare.

The first soldier that was 'helping' Rebecca grabbed at his weapon and spun around as if someone had pushed him. The arms that were holding me instantly broke away, and the man was on the ground completely bewildered.

"Run!" Rippled through the trees as the wind picked up like a breaking storm.

I didn't have to be told twice. Reaching out for Rebecca, I jerked her toward the car, and she seemed to find her thoughts quick enough to throw the keys at me. Quickly we opened the driver's side door and I slid in behind her. Rebecca was sobbing.

"Stop crying, Becs, everything is fine."

"Go, Mary! Go!" She screamed at me.

I didn't have a license, but I did know how to drive. Jerking the car into gear, I pressed on the accelerator and we were off. Rebecca turned around and looked toward the rear of the car.

"I don't see them!" She yelled.

"Calm down," I said. "It's not like they could outrun a car."

Turning in the direction of school, I glanced briefly in the side mirror. There weren't any military lights or sirens blaring.

"Where are you going?" she asked.

"What do you mean? We're going to school."

Our tires spun, as the dirt road ended, and we were on the asphalt that headed to the road into town.

"Are you crazy, Mary? What if they follow us? They know we're going to school."

I sighed. "I doubt it, besides, what are we going to do? If we go to your house, your mom will completely freak out, and my mom will call my dad. He's not the calmest person on the planet. It's not like they know who we are."

"But what about the car? Do you think they'll recognize my mom's car?"

Shaking my head I reached out and grabbed her hand. "Becs, it's okay. I think we should just go to school. Remember what happened to that girl that was raped? They did nothing about it, and then the entire story got turned around. Her whole family was trashed because of it, and who knows where they are now. Nothing happened. We ran into some soldiers, you fell, and so I drove the car to school. Nothing happened."

Her breath slowed more. "Okay, Mary....okay."

"So what made you shout my name?" I asked looking over at her.

Rebecca looked baffled. "I didn't. I just started to run when that thunder boomed out of nowhere. That was crazy, but it made me stop freaking out long enough to think."

Stillness overtook me as she spoke. I had noticed the wind pick up, but I knew I had heard someone call my name. And then who had told me to run? I summed it up as just an inner thought produced by adrenaline. The only thought I had now was to get Rebecca to school and be safe.

The drive was about ten minutes. There wasn't much traffic yet, because it was only around seven o'clock. The best thing for us to do was go to class, not tell anyone about what happened, and just pray. Pray that no one would come looking for us.

Chapter Two

Just left of normal

I'D be lying if I said I could concentrate well. Whatever happened in school that day will always remain a blur. Rebecca seemed to deteriorate as the hours ticked by, and I wasn't sure what we were going to do when school ended.

Around fifth hour I encouraged her to just go to the nurse. She refused to eat lunch, and her complexion was about as pasty as a wall. I knew if we didn't do something, by the end of the day she would crack and tell everyone about what had happened.

Her dad and mom showed up, so her mom could drive her car home, and I prayed as I watched them drive off that she wouldn't say anything. We lived in a society where a man attacking a girl was far too commonplace, and anyone who tried to do something about it, usually ended up worse off.

The situation was even more compounded by the fact that it had been two soldiers. They were known for breaking all the laws they were meant to enforce. Our governmental structure was more than corrupt; it was flat out horrid. Many good men and women had been harassed and some brutalized for going up against the military.

Our current leader was a man named E. Herod. Nobody was even sure what the 'E' stood for, so most times we just called him by the one name. Herod became ruler after his father died, and some even speculated that he had killed him. Ever since I was born, my family spoke about the injustice that had seized the country at his hand.

If Rebecca and I had told anyone about what happened, the local militia would have gone nuts. They were always the subjects of bad reports, but most of the time the people were the only ones that knew their true character. Government officials were content to pay incentives or money to get around the issues, but average citizens didn't have enough to buy our way out of their tactics.

As I closed my locker, I only had two things on my mind. I needed to make sure Rebecca was fine, and then somehow go check on our science project. It sounded crazy, but we only had two more days. In our haste to leave, Rebecca had dropped our log, which had two months worth of information. There wasn't any way that we could reproduce it.

My mother expected me home around four, and the time was three-thirty now. It took twenty minutes to walk home, so the only way to make it would be to ride the bus. I rolled my eyes and headed that direction.

Hordes of teenagers swamped the bus area. It was crazy, but I managed to find bus number twenty-two and step up to the open door. Some kid bumped into me from behind. I fell into the door, but managed to stumble up the stairs in decent form.

I tried to find a seat as close to the front as possible. All sorts of things happened at the back of the bus, and it only took a person one time to make that mistake. Thankfully three rows back was an empty chair, so I sat in it with my face turned toward the glass. This ride would only be ten minutes. I could survive ten minutes.

The noise level increased as the final passengers boarded. Some obnoxious kid sat in front of me, turned and smiled while picking his nose. I rolled my eyes and turned away, and felt the indent of a person sitting on the seat next to me.

I didn't even want to look, but the bus jerked, as it turned out the parking lot. I accidentally leaned too far right. Hesitantly looking up, it was one of whom I called 'the three.' There were three girls intent on punishing every other girl within a mile radius with vicious looks and trash talking. The one-third that I got was named Kim.

"Sorry," I apologized and sat back up closer to the window.

She rolled her eyes. "Yeah, you are," she answered and turned her back toward me.

At least that was all she said. Kim ignoring me was cool. I never got in fights or anything too dramatic, and for the most part I got along with everyone at school. The 'three' pretty much disliked anyone who wasn't a military brat. Why they let civilian and military kids go to the same school no one knew, but most of the time there was an altercation, it usually was in relation to that fact.

I was extremely grateful that my stop was after hers. She got off with a few others about five minutes into our ride, and I scooted over in the seat when she left. Instead of getting off at my usual stop, I planned to get off at the next one to walk quickly to the lake.

If Rebecca knew what I was doing she would probably freak out, but I figured there was no way those guys would still be there. Besides, it was the afternoon and the traffic around the lake picked up after school. I just hoped no one had picked up that logbook.

The bus driver didn't even look at me twice, when I got off

about three stops too soon. After waiting for the bus to leave, I jogged across the road and made my way to the gravel path that led to the lake.

As predicted, there were a few people walking the path, and there were even some cars parked along the grass. I looked around, making sure there were no obvious signs of soldiers, and trotted toward the spot by the water.

I don't know if it was fear, anxiety or anticipation, but I was full of energy when I finally saw the garden spot. Before I even reached it, I could see the bright blue notebook still in the grass, apparently overlooked by anyone going by.

Taking one last look around, I crossed off the gavel path and onto the grass. I bent down and picked up the book. It was in perfect condition, as if we had just laid it there for a moment. Even though she would think I was nuts for retrieving it, I knew Rebecca would be as relieved as I was to get it back.

"Mary." I heard my name whispered.

My heart jumped violently for a moment. I frantically looked around, but the only people I saw were far away. No one was close enough to whisper my name. The wind swirled around me, and the pages of the log flipped in my hand.

Shutting the book tight, I took off my backpack and stuck it inside. I wasn't sure what was going on, but I needed to get home before my mom wondered why I wasn't there right after school.

One last look around and I jogged off in the opposite direction, cutting through the trees and greenery. This was the shortest route to my house, and I had only minutes.

I was used to walking though. For the past three years I'd spent the summers visiting my older cousin Elizabeth on their farm. We'd walk about five miles a day doing hard work, and even though the first few weeks were rather rough, after a month I could keep up with seasoned workers.

As I neared my house, I could see several cars parked in the driveway. My dad must have gotten home a little earlier. We always took him back to work at the mill, and then took my brother and sister to their lessons, but I wasn't sure why the other cars were there.

My brother, Colin, was a math genius. When we did academic testing at school, it was revealed that he had an unusual gift for facts and figures. So even though he was only twelve, the government had mandated that he be put in a training program for the guard. Most parents would have been overcome with pride, but people who believed in the prophecy, believed that the current government would fall. It was foretold that the current system would be overthrown. My parents didn't like that Colin was being trained to be a part of that system.

My sister, Amber, was on the usual path of most girls. She took lessons in manners, dancing and all the preparation for being a good partner to a man. We had a cousin that was married at thirteen, and by my age she already had a child. I wasn't sure what my future held, but the thought of running my own household right now was laughable.

I was about five minutes late, and didn't want my mom to ask me too many questions. She was very observant, so I couldn't figure out how it could be avoided. I opened the gate to walk up the drive, and was never happier than to see my uncle and father come out the front door.

"Uncle Matt!" I yelled and ran up to him.

"Hello, my little Mary." His embrace was always strong and welcoming.

"What are you doing here?" I released him and smiled.

"Well," he said, hesitated and looked at my father. They exchanged some brief, unspoken communication and then he continued. "Your father and I were just discussing some business stuff."

"Hey, dad," I said and gave him a quick hug.

"Hello, kiddo. How was school today?"

I was glad I didn't have to lie. "It was fine. A bit boring." I laughed. "I hardly remember it at all."

They both laughed and my uncle taped my arm. "The answer of most young ladies of fifteen. Soon, you'll have more important things to tend to."

"Mary?" My mother's voice came through the screen.

"Yeah, mom, I'm out here," I answered, still a bit puzzled by my uncle's reference to more important things.

My uncle and father moved over, allowing me through the door. I was surprised to see some of the elders from the meetings we would attend. For a moment my heart shifted, and the only thing I could think was that maybe Rebecca had said something after all. But if that was the case, why was my mother standing in front of me, smiling like she'd won the lottery?

"Mary sweetheart," she began, automatically alerting me. The only time my mother used that endearment was when something important was going on. "We have something very important to talk to you about."

I shook my head. That had to be it. Rebecca told what happened, and now everyone was going to be upset. Both of our families would end up in danger, if we were here to discuss reporting it to the authorities.

While a bunch of crazy thoughts began to enter my mind, I saw Joseph come out of the kitchen with something in his hand. He was dressed really nice, nicer than I'd ever seen him, and for some reason he looked nervous.

"Hey, Mary," he said, his voice sounded a bit muffled.

"Hey," I responded with a nod. I turned to my mother. "What's up, mom?"

She took my hand and led me closer to Joseph. Everyone in the room stood up, and my father walked up beside my mother. Joseph looked like he'd seen something horrific, but somehow he kept his senses about himself enough to say something.

"Mary...I talked to your father."

The room was so still, and I looked back and forth from my mother to my father, completely baffled.

"And what did you talk to my father about?" I asked aloud, but kept my eyes on my parents. My mother instantly looked almost guilty, but my father was beaming with pride.

I felt a weird sensation in my stomach as Joseph stepped closer.

"I asked him if I could marry you, Mary."

Cheers went up throughout the room. My mother embraced me so tight, and I could feel the tears from her face on my neck. While my father was being patted on the back, I looked up to see Joseph's face. It was beet red, but there was a kindness there that was familiar.

I'd known Joseph most of my life, but he was a little older than me. He was a distant cousin from what I understood, and I actually thought he was cute. But cute was a far cry away from husband. I hadn't ever thought about him being my husband.

Married? I felt like something had sucked me out of the room and I was floating. I hadn't thought about getting married. I knew it would eventually come up, but I thought it would be sometime next year or so. My mother hadn't said anything about it

"Oh, Mary," I heard her voice. "You're going to make such a beautiful bride. Your dad and I are so proud of you."

Another embrace and then she darted off to the kitchen. Joseph stepped closer to me, and I realized he was holding out a box in his hand. He opened the lid and I saw a beautiful ring inside.

I heard myself mumble something like 'okay,' and then he slipped it on my ring finger. One year from today we would have a wedding ceremony. No more school, no more playing till after dark with the lightening bugs...I would be getting married?

A squeal of laughter jolted me out of my conversation with self, as my little sister, Amber, grabbed my arm.

"Oh, let me see, Mary." She jumped around so excited I almost forgot what we were talking about. "It's so awesome. I can't wait to tell Leah. She's going to flip, when she hears you're engaged!"

At the word engaged, something in me sucked back into reality. I felt like I'd swallowed a golf ball, and I couldn't take a proper breath in. The weight of this announcement began to settle on my shoulders, and I had to get out of there.

Without regard for who was in the room, I shoved my way through the crowd out the door. I barely registered my mother calling my name as I ran. It didn't matter where I was going, no matter where it was, nothing would change the fact that I was now...engaged.

CHAPTER THREE

SERIOUSLY

I watched the sun go down by the edge of the water. Why I returned to the lake I'm not sure. As I watched the sun get closer and closer to the end of the horizon, I knew I had to inevitably go home.

Married. I guess I knew it was coming, but for some reason it wasn't a preoccupation in my thoughts. So many of my friends were still unmarried at sixteen; I guess I thought it would come up some time next year.

I'd always listened to my parents and done the right thing, and I knew this marriage with Joseph would be very beneficial for the family. My father and he would work out some deal for their business to co-exist within the family, and then responsibility for me wouldn't tax my parents anymore.

Relationship rules were very strict. Guys and girls rarely dated in my culture. Marriages were usually arranged, and it wasn't unusual for distant cousins to marry within a family. I wasn't sure how far removed Joseph was from my family, but all the elders in the room approved.

According to our law, I was actually now Joseph's wife. I was to prove myself pure for a year, and then move into his house. However, because of the issues with the government, today would be seen as an engagement in the eyes of society.

Throwing another rock into the lake, I watched the ripples get wider. I knew my mother would be upset that I had run off, and she was probably completely freaking out the closer the sun went down. Women were rarely alone, especially at night. As evident from what had happened with Rebecca and I today, girls weren't always treated with respect.

"Well," I said aloud standing up. "I might as well face the music."

It took me a few minutes to get home. Even though I didn't want to talk about everything yet, I was relieved to see that Joseph's truck was still there.

Our car was parked in the driveway. The mill was only fifteen minutes from home. My dad owned the machines that the mill rented to get the grain separated, so he had to always be handy in case something went wrong. I figured mom must have dropped him off and returned to make sure I made it home.

Taking a deep breath, I pulled on the screen door and walked in. There wasn't a need for the lights to be on just yet, but my mother had turned on most of the lamps in the living room. The first face I saw was hers, followed quickly by my brother, Colin.

"Where have you been?" My brother's voice was going through that awkward change, so it squeaked at the end.

I turned toward my mother while answering him. "I just went to the lake for a minute. Everything okay?"

I could tell my mother had been crying. I instantly felt horrible for making her cry, but they had to give me a little room for error. I had been completely shocked by their announcement.

"Mary Lynn," she said barely above a whisper. "I drove around for an hour looking for you."

I took off my backpack and quickly knelt down in front of her.

"I'm sorry, mom. I didn't mean to worry you. I was just.... just shocked is all. Everything is okay. I'm okay."

She hugged me so tight, I knew I was instantly forgiven. "I was worried about you, Mary. I know this all seems very sudden, but your dad and I have talked about it for some time. We would never make a choice that would upset you."

I stood up. "It's okay, mom. I really am okay." I rubbed her hand and looked around. "Where's Joseph?"

My little sister bounded into the room. "Hey, drama queen," she teased. "You sure know how to clear a room."

"Amber, there is nothing funny about this," my mother chided her.

Amber laughed. At thirteen and a half years of age, she thought it was very funny. "Sorry mom," she began. "You have to admit though, not many girls get proposed to, and then run for the hills. But then again, you've always said Mary is one of a kind." Smirking, she sat down next to my brother, Colin, who was playing a video game.

My mother stood up and hugged me again and took my hand. "Joseph is in the back, hun. When we couldn't find you, he finished the roof and has been waiting for you to come home."

Letting go of her hand I made my way to the back door. In the distance, I could see a figure at the back of the yard by the fence. What was a person supposed to say to someone they just found out they are going to marry?

He must have heard the door creak, because as soon as I

stepped out on the deck he turned. I couldn't see his expression, but his shoulders became more erect as he walked toward me.

Somehow I got the courage to put one foot in front of the other. We ended up meeting halfway through the yard, and it was the first time that I noticed how much taller he was than me.

His hair was dark brown and a little long in the front. It wasn't enough to cover his eyes, but just enough that the wind blew it across his forehead and above his ears. His eyes were chocolate brown, and he was more tan than usual, from having worked on roofing this past month.

"Hey, Mary," he said softly.

"Hey," I answered, looking everywhere but directly at his face.

"You okay?" He asked.

I paused a moment, surprised at his question. The wind blew rustling the leaves on the trees, and we both turned to look as the last rays of the sun shone through them.

"I'm alright," I finally answered. I walked toward the bench that my father had put in the yard for my mother. Joseph followed me over and stood next to me. I could feel him staring at me, and I had no idea what I was going to say.

I sat down and looked around. Nothing popped into my head. I should want to talk about this, but what was I going to say? *Hey, Joseph, thanks for asking me to marry you?* Thankfully his voice broke the silence.

"Look, Mary. I know this all seems fast, and you were pretty tripped out this afternoon. I'm five years older, and we never hung out much, but I'm a decent guy. I've known your family all my life, and I wouldn't do anything to harm you." He sighed and leaned down closer. "I think I'll be a good husband. My business is doing pretty good, and your dad and I have talked about some joint ventures. I've got a nice house that I started over on Grove Street. I purchased the lot two years ago." He laughed. "I didn't realize it then, but it's really close to here. This way you don't have to be too far from your family."

His voice was so sincere, and it touched me at how tender he was being. I should have known my father and mother would choose someone who I'd only known as kind. I figured my silence was torturing him, so I said the first thing that came to mind.

"Are there trees on the lot?" I asked looking up at him.

Joseph smiled and reached out to take my hand with the ring on it. I had literally forgotten it was even on my finger. I'd never had a guy hold my hand, and an amazingly warm feeling shot through me.

"Yes, Mary. It has tons of trees on it." The warm feeling intensified, and I knew he was staring at me. I wanted to look up, but I couldn't.

He sighed and let go of my hand. "Well, I guess you better get inside. The sun's just about down, and we don't want to start any nasty rumors. We're not officially married yet; don't want to give the neighbors something to talk about."

When he said that I thought about Rebecca. "Oh, wow," I said.

"What?" Joseph asked alarmed.

I laughed. "Oh, it's nothing," I answered and stood up. "I just better get inside and call Rebecca. If she hears it from anyone else, but me, she'll completely freak out."

His expression was perplexed, but he gestured his arm the direction of the house allowing me to pass before him. My sister and mother were at the back door, apparently a witness to our conversation.

"Thank the Creator," my mother said. "Is everything alright?"

"Yes, mom. Joseph and I were just figuring things out. Did you know he's building a house on Grove?"

My sister was excited. "Cool, Mary. You won't be that far at all. Maybe I can come help you sometimes."

I hugged her. "Of course you can, Amber. Hey, where's the cordless? I want to call Rebecca."

"It's upstairs on the hall table," Amber replied.

Turning slightly, but not enough to look at him directly, I waved goodnight to Joseph. He returned my wave with one of his own, as my mother walked him to the front door.

Amber grabbed my arm as we climbed the stairs. "So," she said excitedly. "This will put you guys getting married like in March of next year. Are you going to send out announcements?"

I shrugged. "I don't know. I never really thought about it. I guess mom might want to."

"She's already called half the county." Amber laughed. I loved Amber's laugh. It would be weird not to come home and see her every evening.

"Well, I hope she didn't call Rebecca's mom. Becs will hurt me, if she's not one of the first to know."

Grabbing the phone off the hall table, I went in my room and shut the door. Amber wanted to listen in on my conversation, but I had something else to talk to Rebecca about. I wondered how she was doing after what had happened this morning.

I laid down on my bed, trying to remain calm. Her mom answered on the second ring.

"Hey, Mrs. Levi. This is Mary."

"Oh, hello, Mary." She sounded excited. I knew the cat was already out the bag.

"I was wondering if I could talk to Rebecca?" I asked, disappointed that I would be repeating the news instead of telling her.

Mrs. Levi lowered her voice. "Don't worry," she whispered. "Your mom called and told me, but I knew how important it would be for you to tell Rebecca yourself. She's been asleep most the afternoon, but just got done with dinner. Poor thing, whatever was wrong with her, she must have slept it off."

A huge relief spread through my body as I waited. For one thing, Rebecca hadn't told anyone about today; and her mom hadn't told her about Joseph.

"Hey, Mary." I was relieved that she sounded normal.

"Hey, Becs. You okay?"

"Yeah, no worries." I could tell she was moving into a quieter room. "What about you?"

I sighed. "Oh, I'm alright...I guess." I wasn't sure how to tell her.

"You guess? What's up?" She sounded alarmed.

I hurried with an explanation. "No, it's not about today, I mean not what happened with us today. After school, my parents sort of had a surprise for me. Oh, by the way, I got the logbook for our project."

"Our log? You are nuts, Mary. Please tell me you went back out there with your mom or something."

I laughed. "Uh, yeah. How was I supposed to do that? Probably not the brightest thing to do, considering she would wonder how we left it there. Besides, what I'm about to tell you goes way beyond what happened this morning."

"What?" She sounded like she sucked in a gallon of air.

"It's not bad; it's just...surprising."

"You better spill it now, Mary. I'm about to have a panic attack."

"Alright." I sighed. "When I got home today, there was a room full of people. About five minutes later, I found out that Joseph asked my dad about marrying me."

"Today?" She asked shocked.

"I guess. I'm not sure. All I know is, I have a ring on." I played with the ring on my finger.

"Wow," she said. "I guess I shouldn't be shocked, but you never said anything about liking Joseph. I mean how old is that guy anyway? Didn't he graduate with my brother?"

I'd forgotten that Joseph and Adam had been friends. "I'm not sure, but he's only twenty, silly. Besides, on my birthday this year I'll be sixteen."

She laughed. "Uh, okay. He's still ancient, girl."

"No, he's not. At least he's not ugly or some weirdo." I sat down on my bed.

"Wow," she said. "I guess there's no more playing in the rain for you. You could be somebody's mama by this time next year."

"Shut-up, Becs. That's entirely not possible. It won't be official until this time next year. So if anything, I'll be on a honeymoon somewhere with my husband." As I said the word I cringed, but it wasn't in disgust. I was just surprised at how easily it had come out of my mouth.

"Well, at least you're set. I'm a year older than you, and who knows what my parents are going to do. I don't think anyone's offered to take me." She laughed, but I could tell she was hurt by it.

"I doubt that's possible, Becs. You're one of the prettiest, smartest, and amazing girls I know. Would I lie to you?"

"No." She laughed, but I could tell it was forced. "But, Mary, are you happy? You hardly know Joseph. Is it weird?"

I rolled over on my stomach and looked out the window. The sun had set all the way, and you could see the different streetlights lit on the block.

"I guess it is a little weird, but at least I don't have to wonder who it will be anymore. He seems really nice...even building a house over on Grove."

"Really?" She asked excitedly. "Oh, that's nice, Mary. You won't have to be that far from your family. I hope that happens with me."

"Well," I said sitting up. "You've planned your wedding since we were five. I'm quite sure the Creator will bless you with someone who makes all that planning worth it. You'll probably end up next door to your parents."

"Yeah. That would be so cool."

Thunder rumbled outside, and the smell of rain waif through my open window. I wasn't sure what could ever compare to this moment. I was official engaged, and the world had just gotten so much bigger.

"Hey, Becs?"

"Yeah, Mary."

I got up and walked over to the window. The clouds were rolling in faster, and the wind had picked up. "Are you really okay about today?"

The phone was quiet for a moment. Lightning flashed outside.

"I'm alright. I mean, I was really scared earlier, but you were right. Nothing happened really. We ran into some soldiers, I fell and you drove to school."

"I don't want to make you feel like you're lying or anything, Becs. I just didn't see what good it would do if we told. It would have been a huge mess for our families."

She sighed. "I know. But I'm cool now. Let's just not mention it again. Besides, you've got a wedding to plan."

I sat back down on my bed. "Wow." I giggled. "I seriously have a wedding to plan. This is one of the weirdest, but strangely exciting moments of my life."

"You always have great moments, Mary. You're one of the most blessed people I know. Somehow things just always work out for you. I'm really happy for you, girl."

"Thanks." I looked over at the clock that said almost eight. "I better go. I'm sure everyone will have heard the news by daybreak tomorrow. Nuts, I still need to do my homework."

"What for?" Rebecca asked. "If it were me, I wouldn't bother with school another day. It's not like you'll need to worry about graduating. You'll be hitched before then."

I didn't know how to respond to that. It hadn't dawned on me that I wouldn't be graduating next year. I guess there wouldn't be much point. If I got married in March, it's not like I'd be going back to class.

"Guess I didn't think about that," I almost whispered. "Anyway, I'm going to finish out this year," I offered.

"Aw, Mary, I wasn't trying to bum you out. I was just making a point. Sorry."

"It's alright. I gotta go. Are we walking, riding or driving tomorrow?"

She thought for a moment. "Well, with this rain and mom

working in the morning, I'd say we're up for a bus ride or a soggy walk. Your choice."

"Soggy walk it is," I said decidedly.

Chapter Four

Rain

I had only slept a few hours, completely consumed with thoughts about my engagement. Aside from the obvious shock of just finding out, the weeks and months ahead were full of intrigue. Planning a wedding was going to be interesting.

I had attended several weddings, and it had always been such a fun time. We usually held wedding feast for a week, with all sorts of activities and ceremonies that were significant.

I looked over to the corner where my prayer shawl was thrown across my desk chair. Slipping out of bed, I grabbed it as I slid down to the floor on my knees. This morning seemed like a great opportunity to ask for guidance.

We usually prayed in the privacy of our home. Herod wasn't fond of believers, and though he didn't outlaw worshipping, he didn't encourage belief in any authority other than his own. The militia often taunted believers, and it wasn't a coincidence that many of them were persecuted mercilessly for insignificant things.

This morning I was thankful. Rebecca and I had escaped an ordeal with those men yesterday, and my parents had chosen a husband for me. This union would make things better for us, and I was appreciative that it had been Joseph.

All girls had heard stories of women who got married off to abusive or mean men. Sometimes they were forced to live in horrible conditions. Marriage was not dissolved for any reason that benefited the woman. If a marriage were ending in any other means besides her husband's death, it usually meant the woman would be tarnished for the rest of her life, if she lived at all.

I recited aloud a portion of the prophecy, giving the Creator thanks for all He had allowed. I then thought about the blessed promise, the day the One would come. It had been foretold for ages through my people, that the Creator would come Himself in the form of a man. He would be born to this world, and end up changing the government and the way we had been enslaved to the Herods of this world.

My parents said for years Herod didn't seem to mind people speaking of the prophecy, but something had changed lately. More and more believers were questioned, some even beaten for speaking about the prophecy. Scholars had been predicting the coming the new ruler for years, but it was now that the government began to take notice.

"Mary?" My mother's soft voice rippled through my thoughts.

"Yes, mom." I opened my eyes and turned to see her standing.

"I heard you up already. Are you okay?"

I knew what she was really asking. "Yeah, mom. I'm more than okay." I smiled to let her know that I meant it.

She seemed to relax. "Alright, sweetie. You hungry? I'm going to make pancakes this morning. Your father is still here, if you want to see him. They don't need him at the mill until ten, but he's up already."

I hadn't really thought about my father. The last time I'd seen him was when I'd run out of the house. I sighed. "Sure thing. Let me get ready and I'll be right down."

My mom blew me a kiss and then shut the door. I stood and opened the curtains. The first rays of the sun were just peeking up over the horizon. I knew my father had done the best he could do with accepting Joseph's proposal. I just wish he had given me some kind of heads-up. I knew that men didn't make these types of decisions overnight, and my dad and I were pretty close. He worked a lot of hours, but growing up he always made time for us to talk. I guess this was just a hard subject.

After taking a quick shower and drying my hair, I slipped on a hoodie with jeans. Rebecca and I were walking to school, and it was still a little chilly in the morning. I grabbed my sneakers and backpack then headed down the stairs. I could already smell pancakes and bacon.

"Hey, dad," I said before he noticed I had entered the room.

"Good morning, Mary." He looked relieved. "You alright this morning?"

"Yeah." I sat down on the stool and scooted closer to the counter. "I'm sorry about last night, dad. It was just sort of shocking." I played with a fork that was on the counter.

He sighed. "I know, sweetheart, and I'm sorry about that. I don't know what I figured. It all happened a lot quicker than I thought."

"How so?" I asked as my mom handed me a glass of juice.

"Well," he began. "Joseph talked to me about six months ago, just mentioning the idea. Last month we sort of talked about it again, and I brought it up to your mother. Two days ago he showed us the ring, and before I knew it..." He sighed again. "You were engaged." He looked down at my ring finger.

I spun the ring around. "It's okay, dad, really. Besides, you and mom were in danger of having an old maid around here." I laughed trying to make the sad look leave his face.

"I love you, Mary. We only want what's best for you. Joseph is a really nice young man."

I stood up and hugged him. "I know dad." Leaning back for a second, I then leaned in and rubbed noses with him like when I was little. "And I love you too."

My mom couldn't keep away any longer, a second later we were in a three way hug that I knew was more precious than I had realized. I was growing up, and by this time next year, I would be in my own house, with my own husband.

After a moment my mom squealed. "Oh, no!" She said. "I'm about to burn a batch." She ran over to the stove and began flipping pancakes. My brother entered to mock reprimand her.

"Now, mom. You know I can't eat them if they're the wrong color tan."

"Hush now, Colin. You are so spoiled," she played back.

"Am not," he replied. "But make sure my bacon is nice and crisp too. Last time you had it kind of wobbly."

We all laughed.

"Speaking of wobbly," my dad interjected. We all looked up to see Amber stumbling into the kitchen.

"Good morning," I said.

"Whatever," she replied. Amber had never been a morning person. She was a year younger than I was, and my mother said we were complete opposites.

"Young lady," my mother chided. "Be nice. I thought you'd still be excited about your sister getting engaged yesterday."

Amber looked over at me half sleep. "Old news now, mom. Besides, she might bolt on us before then."

My mother didn't find that funny at all. "Why would you say that?" She looked over at me as if I was hiding something.

Amber laughed. "I'm only kidding mom. Just referencing her Cinderella act from yesterday. I'm surprised she didn't leave a glass slipper behind."

"Ha ha," I interjected with a laugh. "What in the world are you wearing?"

We all looked over at her. She had on her top from yesterday, with an off color pair of jeans and two different shoes.

"I'm not mental, people. Merely a weird dress thing at school today."

My father stood up with his cup of coffee in hand. "School is not like it used to be. We'd have gotten arrested if we wore something like that out of the house."

"Really?" My brother asked.

"Yes," my mom answered. "It would have been seen as rebellious or something." She laughed, but she and my father had told us a ton of stories about how strict things had been thirty years ago.

My sister walked over and grabbed a plate of pancakes. "Well, thank the Creator times are changing. I wouldn't have made it long back then." She wasn't exaggerating. Out of all the girls we knew, she had a streak of being different that sometimes got her in a lot of trouble.

Colin walked over and actually hugged me. For a moment we all stood silent, surprised by his uncharacteristic action.

"I'm going to miss you, Mary," he said sweetly.

I hugged him tighter. "I'm not going anywhere for a whole year, Colin. You'll be sick of me before then."

He let go and looked at me. "No I won't, Mary." He was so serious. I'd never seen him like that before. Most of the time he was either messing around with math figures or playing video games.

My dad laid his hand on his shoulder. "You've still got plenty of time to annoy her, Colin. If you want, I can probably help you with a few ideas."

I rolled my eyes. "Alright, I can see this special moment is over." I let go of my brother. "Hey, mom, can you give me a plate before Amber eats them all?"

Amber stuck her tongue out at me. The phone rang and my dad picked it up. I could tell by the conversation that it was something important. He left the room and everyone began to eat.

About five minutes later he returned. My dad was never the greatest at hiding when something was wrong, but my mother was amazing at acting like she didn't notice.

"I'm going to have to go to work now," he apologized. "I'll call you later to let you know what's up." He kissed my mom on the forehead, and before she could really respond, he was out the door.

We all continued to eat. After fifteen minutes I was done, so I headed up to grab all my stuff for school. I needed to call Rebecca real quick to make sure she was ready to meet me. Being friends with Rebecca was great, but she wasn't the greatest about time.

Her mom answered. "Hello?"

"Hey, Mrs. Levi. It's Mary."

"Oh, I was just about to call you, Mary. Rebecca woke up this morning looking rather worn. She fell back asleep, and I just don't think it's a good idea for her to go to school today. I'm on my way to work, but I'll leave her a note letting her know I told you."

"Sure, uh, okay. I hope she feels better soon."

"I'm sure she will. Have a good day, hun."

The phone was silent immediately, and I clicked the receiver. What in the world was going on? I had just talked to Rebecca last night and she was doing okay. I hope she wasn't upset about the soldiers after all.

I walked to my room and set the cordless phone on the hall counter. The only thing yuckier than walking in the mud to school: walking in the mud to school alone. However, anything was better than having to ride the bus. If I left now, I would have plenty of time to get to school.

The timing of thunder couldn't have been more poetic. I went back to my room to see a downpour of rain, thick enough for you to have trouble seeing across the street. It figured though. March and April always poured around here, sometimes without notice.

I went to the bathroom, determined to pin my hair up and brave the monsoon. My hair was so thick, long, and would be all over the place if left untied. I brushed it quickly and made a single braid on the side. At least this way, I could keep it all under a ball cap. Combined with an umbrella, I should make out okay by the time I made it to school.

Grabbing my huge umbrella out of the closet, I headed downstairs.

"Kind of early for the bus, isn't it, Mary?" My mother walked toward me with a smile and a dishtowel.

"Just a bit," I admitted. "I was thinking about braving the torrent."

She shook her head. "I don't think that's such a good idea. It's really coming down." Walking past me to the front door, she opened it and the sound of thunder echoed loudly.

I walked up beside her. "Well, I'd have to say it doesn't look like it's letting up, but I really don't want to ride the bus."

"I tell you what," my mom offered. "You want me to go ask Mrs. Smithers next door to take you on her way to the shop?" She owned the local grocery store.

"No, that's okay, mom. I really think I'll be fine. It's not like it's that far anyway. Besides, it looks like it might be slacking up." Just at that moment a ray of sunlight filtered through the street, and it seemed to ease up a little.

"Well, alright. Just call me when you get to the office; let me know you made it okay."

"Will do. Love you, mom." I gave her a kiss on the cheek and stepped out into the rain.

At least it wasn't a cold rain, and the wind wasn't blowing too badly. I waved one more time to my mom, before she closed the door, and headed off down the street. A few cars went past me, but I stayed far enough away from the street not to get splashed. I figured it would take me just fifteen minutes and I'd be at school.

About five minutes into my walk, a horn beeped shortly. I looked over my left shoulder to see a familiar truck. While I had seen it a hundred times, I hadn't expected to see Joseph this early in the morning. He rolled down the passenger side window of the truck and yelled out.

"Hey, Mary!"

I waved and stepped over to the truck door. "What are you doing?" I asked, peering in the window.

Instead of answering me, he got out and came around the front of the truck. He was getting soaking wet in the rain.

"I saw your dad a minute ago. He said you and Rebecca would probably need a ride to school. Your mom said you had just left by the time I got there." Opening the truck door, he extended his hand to help me get in.

"Thanks," I said, hopping up the step onto the seat. The roughness of his hand was memorized on my fingers. He shut the door behind me and ran around the truck to get in. I wiggled the ring on my finger.

"You good?" He asked and slammed the door beside him.

"Yeah, thanks," I answered, trying not to seem tense. This was the first time I'd ever ridden with Joseph in his truck. It was old, but he had taken good care of it.

"Are you cold?" He asked, fumbling with the knobs on his dashboard.

"No," I said and shook my head. "I'm good." I really didn't know what else to say.

We rode for a moment in silence before he finally spoke.

"I figure we've got a year to hang out and get to know each other," he said very matter of fact, but kind.

I shrugged. "I guess that's one way to get straight to the point." I responded.

"Sorry," he apologized. "I've never done this before, and I'm trying to make it less awkward for you."

Blowing out the breath I hadn't realized I was holding, I responded in a rush of words. "Joseph, it's okay. I just have to get used to the idea, that's all. I didn't mean that weird, it's just...well, I don't know." My voice trailed off almost in a tear. I couldn't look over at him. My whole world had changed yesterday. How was I supposed to feel?

"I know this is a bit weird for you still, Mary. But just so you know, I'm really grateful that you accepted my proposal."

I tried to stifle my snicker, but it escaped. "Proposal?" I asked.

"Yeah," he responded. I glanced over as he turned with a weird look on his face.

"If I remember correctly, "I offered. "I don't recall you actually asking me a question."

Joseph looked at me a little stunned, and I turned my attention back to the rain. I didn't have any idea why I said that, but I wasn't one for not speaking the truth of what I thought.

"Well," he started, but paused so long I thought he'd lost track of what he was going to say.

"It's okay, though," I said.

He raised his hand to cut me off. "No." He shook his head. "It's not okay, Mary." Joseph sighed and stopped the truck. We weren't quite to school yet, and I was completely confused as he got out and walked around the front of the truck.

Opening my side door, Joseph smiled at me as he took my hand and knelt down. He was getting drenched by the rain, not to mention the huge puddle he was now in.

"Mary Lynn Meir, I've got a question for you," he stated loudly above the thunder.

"Yes?" I responded with a smile.

"Will you marry me?" He all but shouted, because the rain and thunder had considerably picked up within seconds.

Water poured down his face, soaking his shirt and jeans. I noticed the stubble on his face beneath a perfect smile, and my heart melted.

"I believe I will, Joseph...uh, wow! I don't know what your middle name is!" I shouted above the downpour.

"Matthew! It's Joseph Matthew!" He shouted even louder. "I'm named after your uncle Matt!"

"Oh! I didn't know that!" I hollered. "Well, Joseph Matthew Abrams, I think I will marry you!"

I was completely unprepared for what he did next. Joseph yelled really loud, suddenly jumping up off of his knees. Water was dripping off his entire body, but he didn't care. He smiled at me so adoringly and then shut the door. The look on his face as he went back around to his side of the truck was priceless. I didn't know much about this man, but what I was learning was really sweet.

I played with the ring on my finger again. Maybe everything was going to be okay. Being Mrs. Mary Lynn Abrams wasn't going to be such a scary thing after all.

CHAPTER FIVE

WHAT IS WILL BE

OF course everyone knew about Joseph and I. The majority of my school didn't believe in arranged marriages, so my engagement was some serious news. It probably escalated the conversation, when Joseph got out of his truck and let me out right in the front of school. He stood there in the rain, getting even wetter, and waited until I had gone all the way into the building.

"Hey, Mary," my friend Dianna said, almost tackling me.

"Hey," I responded, trying to balance myself.

"Let me see it." She jumped around like she had to pee.

"See what?" I laughed and took a step down the hallway.

"See what?" She looked at me like she wanted to slap me. "The ring, of course."

I knew what she was talking about, but teasing Dianna was more fun than teasing my sister, Amber.

"Oh, alright." I smiled and held my hand out for her to see.

She gasped. "Wow, that is gorgeous. I can't believe this, Mary. You are actually going to be someone's wife!" The last of her words seemed to bounce off the ceiling. A few people in the hallway were obviously as curious as she was.

"I know," I answered. "It's not like the wedding is next week though, silly. I've got an entire year of still being just a girl."

Dianna laughed. "Yeah, just a girl who is fifteen, engaged to a dude who is twenty, and not just any dude, one of the finest dudes in the town."

Shaking my head I walked with her down the hall. I felt my face get hot, and a lump formed in my throat. Tears welled up in my eyes, but I fought them off.

"You okay, Mary?"

I nodded, realizing that my voice would betray me and I'd have to explain. But how could I explain what I was feeling?

She rubbed my back as we walked. "Hey, it's not like you're some freak. There have been plenty of girls throughout the years that got married young. Although most of them were knocked up or something, but it's not like you are...right?"

Her question forced the emotions out of me.

"Are you seriously asking me that?" I turned to her and a tear rolled down my face.

Dianna immediately looked remorseful. "Oh, Mary, I didn't mean to hurt you. I wasn't saying I thought that. Some people were asking, and you have to know by now, your reputation stands good all by itself. No one would believe such a nasty rumor even for a second. I know your people tend to get married young, and I really don't see why it's such a big deal."

"So people are already saying stuff like that?" I asked looking around.

She shrugged. "People are people, girl. They talk about you no matter what because they're bored. I'm not being funny, but when's the last time you heard about anyone getting engaged at fifteen? It'll all blow over though, so don't worry about it."

We entered the hallway where our lockers were, and I could

see my locker decorated outside with hearts and diamonds. I immediately felt better.

"Oh, Mary!" My friend Flower shouted. "You are so blessed!"

"Thanks, Flower," I said and walked over.

She extended a beautiful yellow rose from behind her back. "I wouldn't be true to my name, if at an occasion like this, I didn't give you a flower."

I took the rose and hugged her. "Thank you." I sighed. "It's been an interesting twenty-four hours."

Flower was the daughter of one of my mother's best friends. We had grown up together, and I still remember the first day I learned what her name was. I was only five, so it took me a while to understand that Flower was her name and not an object.

"Well, don't be upset, Mary. Not everyone understands our culture. Those that do are very happy for you, and I can only hope I'll be announcing my own engagement within the next year."

"But at least you're already sixteen," I responded.

Dianna hugged me. "But you'll be sixteen in November. No one will care much after that. What's the average age for y'all to get married anyway?"

"I'd say about seventeen or eighteen, for the actual marriage. I've heard of girls getting engaged as young as fourteen before, but most don't get married that young." I looked over to Flower for support.

"Yeah," she said with a nod. "I think most get engaged around sixteen or seventeen though." Flower smiled at me. "But our Mary was always exceptional and anything but average."

I laughed. "At least I have a year." I linked my arm in with

Flower's. "So we've got months to act like average teenagers."
They both laughed.

The bell rang, so I quickly hugged them and ran to class.
I wasn't so sure how this day was going to unfold, but I had a
sense of anticipation. My friends had totally helped me feel at
ease about the situation, and as I felt the weight of the ring on
my finger, I gained confidence that everything would be more
than okay.

The day went on as usual. There were a couple of stares and
whispers, but for the most part no one said much to me about
the engagement. I wondered by fourth hour how Rebecca was
doing. When school was out I would go by and see her.

I figured she hadn't told anyone a thing about yesterday,
because her parents or mine would have been up here talking to
me. I didn't have to be right home after school, so I planned to
just walk to her house and see what she was up to.

"Hey, gypsy slut," a voice said behind me.

I turned to see Kim, Katrina and Katherine, with a couple
of their friends at the next table. Instead of responding, I just
turned back around. Dianna and Flower were on their way over
to my table, so I scooted over.

"Hairy Mary," she taunted. "Now that you're getting
married, are you allowed to shave your legs?" A burst of laughter
erupted from her friends.

"Shut-up, Kim." Flower's voice was loud in my defense.

I didn't need to turn around to see Kim's face with her
response. "Are you talking to me gypsy? What's your real name
anyway?"

Flower sat down at the table and reached across to grab my
hand. "Ignore her, Mary. She's just jealous. The last man that

paid any attention to Kim was her audiologist. And that was only because he had to listen."

Dianna laughed so hard she choked on her drink, and Flower let go of my hand to pat her on the back.

"That was funny," Dianna spurted out around her coughs.

From behind us Katrina's voice sounded nasty. "They can form sentences. Must be a stellar day for the believers."

At the word believer I tensed. This did not need to become a conversation about beliefs. The last time that happened, a few people got suspended from school.

Flower's voice was still cheerful. "It is a stellar day for us," she responded. "My amazing friend, Mary, is engaged to be married. That's married, not hooked up in the back of Steve Zeller's truck."

Simultaneous gasps echoed behind me, and I tried to stifle my laugh. Flower had just hit a sore spot with Katrina for sure. She didn't have the best reputation.

"Whatever," Katherine said defensively. "Shut your mouth Flower Power, before I have to come over there and do it for you."

Tension would be the lesser word. I felt this getting out of hand, so I turned around.

"Hey, let's just drop it." I nodded over to the cafeteria monitor. Everyone turned. "I'm not trying to get red-carded at the end of the school year. Let's just drop it." With that I turned around. The table behind me didn't respond openly, but I could feel fire on my back with their stares.

Dianna leaned forward. "Nice save," she whispered. Just at that moment I looked up and saw the monitor walking toward the table. He passed without saying anything to us.

"Just think, Mary," Flower began. "By this time next year,

you won't have to deal with stupid girls, stupid monitors or stupid school."

"I like school," I admitted. "I'll miss it...and you all."

Dianna smiled. "It's not like you're going to your death. We'll still all see each other. Well, I mean, as long as Flower doesn't get engaged and be forced to move out of town or something."

Flower shook her head. "Not possible. My parents are already looking at some guy in the neighborhood."

"What?" I exclaimed. "You didn't tell me."

She laughed. "There's nothing to tell, really. I overheard them talking about it a couple of weeks ago. They have no idea I know. I figure mom will have 'the talk' with me soon, and then I'll know. And it's about time. At seventeen with no engagement, I was beginning to get self-conscious." We all laughed.

Lunch was over and we headed to our classes. I was excited because our science project was looking to be one of the best. Rebecca and I had developed our own seeds by crossbreeding at the lake, and they were actually growing. Now, all we had to do was compare them to the things we had grown at school and we'd be done.

Our school was big on agriculture. The greenhouse out back was magnificent, and I loved spending time out there. I explained to Mr. Prescott that Rebecca wasn't feeling well, but assured him our project would be right on time. He excused me to go out to the greenhouse, so I gathered my things and headed to the back of the school property.

The greenhouse wasn't attached to the school building, so I put up my hoodie and umbrella before walking out. The rain was still falling fast, but I jogged the quick distance in no time.

Lowering my umbrella I walked in. I loved being out here.

The only sound was the rain falling against the glass above, and I watched as streaks of water ran down the sides of the greenhouse to the ground outside.

This building was pretty long, and some people found it creepy to be out here alone. I clicked on the solar powered lamps, and made my way further back into the building. I knew no one was here, so I would always sing while I analyzed our project.

Today I wasn't exactly in a cheerful or sad mood, so the song I found myself humming was something from one of the prophecies. I didn't say the words aloud, but the words echoed in my heart as I hummed.

When I reached our project, I clicked on the lamp in the corner so I could see it clearly. It had grown really well, but looked nothing like the amazing seedling that Rebecca and I had down by the lake. There was something about the water there that made ours grow incredibly well over the last month.

Retrieving the logbook from my bag, I jumped as a huge round of thunder shook the building. Lightning must have hit somewhere really close, and I looked around the greenhouse to make sure it hadn't hit the building.

"Mary," I heard a voice speak within the thunder.

Frantically I looked around. The lights I had turned on earlier seemed to dim as the rain picked up, and my heart beat hard in my chest.

"Who is it?' I asked and backed up toward a table of plants.

Instantly the rain increased, thunder rumbled throughout the greenhouse, and I felt myself yelling. It was so loud I couldn't hear my own voice above the thunder.

All of a sudden, all noise was sucked out of the room. Wind

flew all around me, and things were flying in the air though they didn't touch me.

"Mary, do not be afraid," the voice said.

I looked up, and a bright shaft of light was coming toward me. All I could think was that lightning was about to strike the greenhouse. My voice vibrated out my mouth, though I couldn't hear it, and I fell to the floor. Preparing for the glass that would inevitably be shattered on top of me, I covered my head and yelled.

"Mary," a kind voice said. "Do not be afraid, child. The Creator has found favor on you this day."

I felt the heat of him before I saw him. Slowly I lifted my head. There before me was the form of a man incased in brilliant light. The energy radiating from him was pulsing, but somehow I knew it was soft. For some reason I reached out my hand, and light filtered through my fingers.

Sitting up all the way on my knees, I was beholding the most amazing creature I had ever seen. The more I looked, the clearer he came into focus. Glorious details of his face emerged as he spoke.

"Hello, Mary, highly favored one."

Somehow I realized I had stopped yelling. My thoughts made it out my mouth.

"Favored one? What are you talking about? Who are you? What are you?" My lips trembled as the words stumbled out.

The being smiled. "Do not be afraid, Mary; for you have found favor with the Creator. You will conceive in your womb a son and you will name him Jesus. He will be great, and will be called the Son of the Most High."

I held my hands up as the brilliant light washed over me.

I clearly heard the words he spoke, but they didn't make any sense.

"But," I began hesitantly. "How can I have a baby? I haven't even kissed a guy, let alone had sex."

Light shot all around as he answered, "The Holy Spirit will come upon you, and the power of the Most High will overshadow you; the holy offspring will be called the Son of the Creator."

My entire body began to shake. I felt tears fall down my face, and the being got nearer to me. He reached out his hand and I put my small hand in his. He smiled.

"Mary, even now your cousin, Elizabeth, is pregnant in her old age. She was infertile, but now is within her sixth month. Nothing is impossible with the Creator."

He helped me stand to my feet as his words ended. Warmth spread throughout my entire body, and I felt like I was floating. The light emitting from his body was warm, and I was no longer afraid. I knew this being...this angel, had been sent from the Creator. The prophecy of the new leader became reality... my reality.

"I'll do it," I whispered. "Let it all happen the way you have said."

As soon as the last word escaped my mouth, a burst of light shot through the entire greenroom. All of a sudden I could hear the thunder and the rain again. It pounded down furiously on the glass roof of the greenhouse. A beautiful sound of music rang throughout the air, and the angel before me beamed brighter.

In an instant he was gone. The dimness of the room was shocking, as if I was rendered blind, but it was just the absence of the glorious light. I fell to my knees again, shaking with the tears that ran down my face.

Instinctively I placed my hand on my abdomen. I was the one. The one that the prophecies foretold would carry the Child. The Son of the Creator would be born here on earth to a virgin mother, and that mother was me.

It wasn't unbelief that paralyzed me; it was shock. My entire life I had been told the story. My parents had sang and told testimonies of the prophets, and how our Redeemer was soon to come.

And what had he said about Elizabeth? She and her husband Zachariah had been unable to have children all these years. She was well over fifty now, but the angel said she was six months pregnant. How could this be?

I grabbed the table next to me and pulled myself up. My face felt so flush, like when you've been out in the sun too long. But inside of me, there was a newfound hope. I couldn't comprehend what had just happened, but I understood what I had been told.

A crack of thunder echoed above me, and lightening flashed illuminating the greenhouse. I wasn't sure how much time had passed, but I figured someone might come looking for me soon. I gathered my things, stuffed them in my backpack and clicked off the lamp. Walking slowly, I took each step with wonder.

The greenhouse looked completely normal. All the things that had appeared to be flying around in the air were stable, and I was in awe of how different the room had looked moments ago. I put my backpack on my shoulder as I made it to the entrance of the greenhouse. Turning around, I looked back the way I had come, but the angel was gone.

Leaning up against the doorframe, I wiped fresh tears from

my face. It was then that I noticed the gold ring that glittered from the reflection in the light. A weight went across my chest, and I felt like I would be sick. When was all this going to happen? This child would be the Son of the Creator, so how would that factor into me marrying Joseph? If I had a baby before he and I were married, that was grounds for excommunication. Worse than that, the ancient laws called for the execution of a woman found committing adultery.

I took a deep breath and sighed. I had to believe that everything would somehow be okay. The angel had said Elizabeth was pregnant. She believed in the prophecies, and was my closest relative. I needed to talk to her, but I didn't want to do it over the phone. I needed to get there in person.

As I stepped out into the weather, the rain slackened. Tiny rays of sunlight peered through the clouds, and I felt a sense of unexpected peace. As I walked, I felt as if someone was beside me. I don't know how to explain it other than that; I just didn't feel alone anymore.

CHAPTER SIX

CROSSROADS

I had no idea how to make it to Elizabeth's house. She lived about two and a half days by bus, so it's not like I could just go on the weekend and be right back. We still hadn't taken finals in school yet, and my mom and dad were expecting me to stay here this summer to help at the mill.

The angel had said she was six months already, so her baby would be due around June. I wondered why she hadn't told any of the family about her pregnancy. Mom would have been so happy for her, but I guess they wanted to make sure everything was going to be okay before they told everybody.

The final bell rang and I came out of the school building. I was shocked to see him. Joseph was parked a little way down from the building, but I could see his beaming smile just beyond the crowd.

A little fire felt like it had been lit inside of me, and then every time I encountered him it grew even more. Who was this man, this man who would within a year be my husband? And now, what was he going to say when he learned that I was to be the mother of the Creator in the flesh?

I wasn't sure how to even tell anyone, or if I was supposed to. Obviously there would come a time when I couldn't keep it

a secret, but today didn't seem like a good time to start telling
everyone.

"Hey, Joseph," I greeted him and smiled.

"Hi, Mary. Hope you don't mind me coming. Your mom
said you really don't like riding the bus, and with all the rain, I
figured you'd walk." He smiled and opened the truck door for
me.

"Thanks, I do appreciate it." I didn't want him to think
I didn't want a ride, but I would have rather been alone right
now. I felt like my mind was going to explode. The sooner I was
alone, the better.

He started the truck and veered off into traffic. For some
reason I scooted over as far away from him as possible, and after
a moment I realized I had my hand on my stomach. Quickly I
moved it and glanced over to see if he noticed.

Joseph really was handsome. He had changed his clothes
from this morning, and there wasn't much evidence of our early
morning drive. The blue shirt he had on now sort of matched
the outside of his truck, and his jeans were faded.

Even though he slightly held the steering wheel, the muscles
in his arms and hands were very pronounced. I'm sure this was
true for most contractors. In the past my dad had taken me to
see houses that Joseph had built from the ground up, so I knew
he was very skilled at his craft.

"Mary?" He asked so weirdly, it must have not been the
first time.

"Yeah," I replied, as a hot flash of embarrassment washed
over me.

"You okay?" He looked at me with genuine concern.

"Yeah," I answered again, this time attempting to engage.

"Well, I was asking you how school went today. Everything go alright?"

I nodded. "Classes were good." *And an angel visited me in the greenhouse.*

"Oh, that's good," he responded. "You only have two more months of school, then what? Are you going to Zachariah's place?"

That was an interesting question. Maybe this conversation was going in the right direction.

I turned toward him. "Well, this year my dad needs me to work at the mill in June, so I'm not able to go to Elizabeth's for the three months like usual."

"I thought Zachariah did his harvest earlier than that. Didn't you go at the end of April last year?"

"Beginning of May, actually. I only missed about two weeks of school."

He paused, waiting for a car to pass, then looked back over at me. "You and Elizabeth were always really close weren't you?"

"Yeah. She's more like my second mom than a cousin. She and Zachariah are much older, so they don't travel here like they used to," I admitted. "I really miss them. After the wedding, I'm sure I won't get as much time to go see them."

Awkward isn't the appropriate word, but it's the closest I could get to what I felt. I was actually planning my future with a man to be married, while probably pregnant with a baby. This was beyond awkward.

Joseph smiled at me as we pulled up to my house. "Well, maybe there's a way you can go out there earlier. I'm sure your mom and dad won't mind, as long as you're back in time to help at the mill."

"Brilliant!" I shouted and leaned toward him. I could have

hugged him, but it would have been almost absurd. The guy had only touched my hand twice. Instead, I patted him on the shoulder and smiled. "Thanks, Joseph."

He smiled even bigger and laughed. "You're welcome, Mary. Hey, tell your mom I'll be over in thirty minutes to finish the awning. I'm going over to Clifton to check on my guys."

"Alright, I will. See you later?" I asked more than declared.

"Absolutely," he said with a grin.

I ran from his truck through the gate and entered the front door. I had wanted to go see Rebecca, but after the visit from the angel, I wasn't so sure that was a good idea. I needed time to think; to be alone for a moment.

"How was school, Mary?" My mother's cheery voice was always a comfort.

"It was fine, mom," I replied, trying to act as normal as possible.

"Why, Mary, you look....like you're glowing. Does this have to do with your ride home from school today?"

I put my hand across my stomach. "I'm fine, mom. Joseph was talking to me about visiting Elizabeth."

She frowned. "Oh, I'm sorry, sweetie. I know how you wanted to go this year, but we need everyone's help to get this job done."

Shaking my head I sat down on the couch. "No, I know. I was planning on doing that. It's just, well, Joseph had a great idea. What if I still got to spend my three months with Elizabeth like usual?"

She frowned again. "Mary, we've already discussed this. Everyone in the family is needed this year."

"Oh, I know, mom." I smiled and she looked even more confused.

"What are you talking about then?" She asked sitting down next to me.

"Okay, what if I went to see them sooner, and then was home by June?"

My mother shook her head. "That won't work, what about school?"

I shrugged. "It's not like I'm going to end up graduating traditionally anyway. Now that I'm getting married, I plan on just getting my GED next year."

This time she squinted her eyes at me, like she was searching for something. I looked directly at her, intent on her perceiving only my desire to go see Elizabeth.

"And you've talked about this with Joseph?"

"Yeah," I answered. "Actually, it was his idea." It was so nice to be able to say that.

She leaned back on the couch. "Well, you'd have to leave fairly soon. I don't know that your father and I have the money to get you there and back, honey."

I jumped up. "Thank you, thank you, thank you!"

My mom stood up and touched my arm. "Now wait a minute. I didn't say yes. I said I don't think we have the money."

"But I have it from last year's birthday. Plus Uncle Matt gave me two hundred dollars for Christmas. That's more than enough for me to pay my way there and back on the bus."

When there was only silence, I knew I had won the debate. This was somehow working out so brilliantly, and I was ecstatic.

"Your father will want to weigh in on this, Mary. Don't get too excited." She let go of my arm and went toward the kitchen. "I don't have a problem with it as long as he doesn't. Hey, wait a minute," she said turning back toward me. "Have you even considered that Elizabeth and Zachariah might not be ready to have you come so early?"

I shook my head. "What's there to get ready? I sleep on a cot in an extra room, and right about now they're getting some of their harvest stuff done anyway. It will be alright mom."

"But they won't even know you're coming in time. They still don't have a phone out there, and you might get there before a letter did." She looked concerned.

Walking over to her I smiled. "Mom, I'm sure it's not a big deal. We know they are there, and it will be a nice surprise for them. Besides, this is probably the last year I'll get to go out there for awhile." I held up my ring in the light.

"Okay, Mary. I'll talk to your dad tonight when he gets home. Are you sure about missing out on school like this?"

I walked back over to retrieve my stuff from the couch. "Yes, without a doubt. I really want to go see her mom, and I'll be back to help dad."

My mother walked off into the kitchen, and as I went to the stairs I heard her humming. Humming or singing in my house always meant happiness. I climbed the stairs and went into my room. My hoodie was a little damp from being out in the rain so much today, so I took it off and left it on the floor. Untying my hair, I went into the bathroom. There was a full-length mirror on the back of the door, so I shut it and did a quick observation.

My stomach looked the same as it had this morning. I turned sideways and looked again, gently rubbing down past my navel. I didn't know much about pregnancy, but I figured there wouldn't be a way to tell just yet. I wasn't sure if the angel meant I was pregnant now, or if I would be soon.

There was a tiny window in my bathroom nearer the

ceiling. I looked out to see the rain falling harder again, and I thought about the last forty-eight hours of my life. Everything had changed.

After kicking off my shoes, I slid my jeans off onto the floor. My robe was hanging on a hook nearby, so I grabbed it and tied the belt around my waist. Lightening flashed outside, and the light flickered in the bathroom and then went out.

I leaned up against the wall and stared out at the rain. The tiny window provided just enough light to see my hand as I held it up in front of me. The ring Joseph had given me was simple, yet beautiful. The thin gold band perfectly fit my finger, and the diamond on top was astounding. Usually people in my culture didn't put jewels on engagement rings, but my mother must have hinted to Joseph that I liked diamonds. It wasn't flashy, but I wouldn't use the word modest either.

What in the world was going to happen now? I rested my hand with the ring on my stomach. I was the mother of the Son of the Most High. I was going to have a baby. A baby that was entering the world by supernatural means, and there wouldn't be one person I could think of who would believe me.

Panic seized me as the rain picked up outside. I slid down the wall to the floor and began to sob. Why me? Why had the Creator chosen me for this honor? Why now? The prophecy had been talked about for generations, but mine was the apparent chosen one? What if something went wrong? What did I know about babies anyway?

I was glad the rain was so loud and the lights were out. I cried until the tears stopped flowing, and even then I sobbed. My entire life was spinning out of control, and there was nothing I could do to stop it. For that matter, there was nothing I wanted to do to stop it. Carrying the child of the Creator was a humbling honor, and the more I thought about marrying Joseph, the more this burning feeling grew within me.

*****

A knock on the bathroom door alerted me that I had fallen asleep.

"Mary?" It was my sister, Amber.

"Yeah," I answered, realizing the lights were back on.

"Mom said dinner's ready."

"Alright. I'll be out in a minute," I replied.

Her steps sounded lighter as she left my room. I wasn't sure how long I had been asleep. I stood up and looked in the mirror. My long brown hair was strewn all over the place, so I grabbed a brush and then tied it into a ponytail.

My eyes were a bit puffy, but some cold water would soon remedy that. I turned on the facet and splashed water on my face, until I felt my skin tighten from the coldness. After drying my face I opened the door. There really wasn't a need to get dressed. The clock on the dresser said it was already seven thirty, no wonder my sister had come banging on the door.

I slipped my feet into slippers and headed downstairs. My mom, brother and sister were in the kitchen eating at the table.

Amber loved to tease me. "Well, if it isn't Sleeping Beauty."

"Ha, ha," I responded and grabbed a plate.

"You fell asleep?" My mother asked, immediately concerned.

I shrugged. "When the lights kicked off, so did I. It's been an exhausting couple of days though, don't you think?" I winked at her.

"Of course, honey. Here, get some mashed potatoes." She piled them high on my plate.

Colin handed me a piece of paper. "Check this out, Mary. I got all A's and the highest marks in the class."

I read the grades on his report card and smiled. "Wow, Colin, you're pretty smart." I handed it back to him.

"Did you get your report card yet?" He asked with a smile.

Rolling my eyes I reached for the green beans. "Not yet, and no, I didn't get straight A's."

Amber laughed. "Well, you can't be completely perfect, Mary. What about your science project? Do you and Rebecca have that finished yet?"

"Yeah," I answered before taking a huge bite of meatloaf.

The kitchen door opened and I almost swallowed my tongue along with the meat.

"Sorry to interrupt dinner," Joseph apologized.

I closed the top of my robe, immediately aware that I didn't have clothes on underneath it.

My mother stood up to greet him. "Oh, it's no interruption, Joseph. Did you get finished?"

"Yes," he answered her, but glanced over at me. I felt my entire body light on fire.

Colin chimed in. "How did you do all that with so much rain?"

Joseph smiled, but it wasn't as authentic as usual. "There wasn't much to it really. I just had to nail up some stuff for the gutters at the back of the house." When he said the back of the house, he looked over at me. Concern was in his eyes.

I looked down and took another bite of my food. When I looked up, my mother was looking at me with a peculiar look.

"Uh, Mary, you might want to excuse yourself for a minute. I was going to invite Joseph to sit and eat with us, but one of us is a bit underdressed." She nodded at me.

Flames from within leapt around my entire body, and without a word I left the table and ran up the stairs. Quickly, I put on a shirt with some sweatpants. Mortified, I slowly made my way back toward the kitchen.

Joseph was still there, and my mother had obviously seated him right next to me. Thankfully no one said anything when I returned, but I did notice my little brother laughed, and then my mom gave him a look that made him stop.

Sitting back down, I kept staring at my plate like it was a Renoir painting. My mother had started a conversation about the trees in the yard, and my sister was prattling on about how she should never cut one down.

After a moment, I realized Jospeh was staring at me. My knee bounced up and down beneath the table, and I couldn't figure out why he was just looking at me. Everyone else was engrossed in some silly conversation about preserving or chopping down stuff in the yard, and all I wanted to do was ask him why he was looking at me.

Joseph finally relieved my suffering.

"Is it alright if I talk to you in private?" He asked me, causing all the conversation at the table to stop.

I took a drink of my soda. "Yeah, sure."

He stood and I scooted my chair back from the table. My mother looked at me with questioning eyes. I shrugged, communicating that I had no idea what he wanted.

We made our way back to the little office that my father had at the house. The door was open, so Joseph reached in and clicked the lamp on.

"Is this okay?" He asked, so concerned I got anxious.

"Um, hmm," I responded quickly.

He extended his hand so I would know to have a seat on

the little couch, and he took the chair from my father's desk. Pulling it up in front of me, Joseph sat down and sighed.

"Mary, first, let me just say that I know all of this is really crazy for you."

I didn't respond. Not one muscle of my body moved, but my chest felt tight.

"I've liked you for awhile now, but knew my proposal had to wait for the proper time. I know people of our culture get married even younger at times, but I prayed to the Creator and felt it His will for me to wait until you were sixteen."

The more he talked, the more my chest felt like it would burst.

"And even though I have feelings for you, I don't want to make you unhappy. If you don't want to marry me, I will let you out of the agreement."

I felt like I'd been slapped in the face. He sat there in front of me waiting for a response, but I don't think even I expected what came out my mouth.

"Let me out of the agreement?" I felt my world crumbling. "You don't want me... to marry you?" A sob surfaced and I felt miserable.

Joseph's face displayed so many emotions at once. I couldn't tell what he was thinking.

"No, Mary, it's not that." He stood and paced the room. "I heard you today. I heard you crying, while I was fixing the awning at the back of the house. I can't bear it, I can't be the cause of you grieving like that." He sat down on the chair and took both my hands. "I'd rather be alone the rest of my life, than make you do something you don't want to do."

My tears gave way to my heart. This man kneeling before

me loved me. I'd never seen it before, but there was no doubt what he was saying and emitting now.

"Joseph," I whispered. "It's not that...it's not you."

Softly he stroked my hand. "What is it then? Do you just want to wait longer?"

I shook my head. "No, I mean..." What was I going to tell him? "It's not that. I just need some time to think."

He leaned in closer to my face. "Are you sure, Mary? Are you sure that's all it is? I'm in no rush. If you want to make the engagement two years we can. Is it school? Do you want to graduate with your class?"

For some reason I laughed. "School is the least of my concerns, Joseph."

He reached over to the box on the desk and then handed me a tissue. "Well, what is concerning you? You are part of my life now, and I want to help you however I can."

Hysterical laughter shook my body, and for a moment he almost look frightened.

"Help me?" I laughed. "I don't think that's possible, Joseph. Not even for someone who obviously cares about me so much."

He looked so concerned then, I regretted saying it.

"But what is it? Did someone do something to hurt you? I've never heard anyone cry the way you did today, Mary. Honestly, tell me."

I hadn't realized I was so vocal today in the bathroom. The thunder had been so loud, and I didn't know he was working on the awning.

"Joseph, did you say you prayed to the Creator and felt this was His will, you and I married?"

He nodded. "Yeah." A huge smile spread across his face.

"Then everything will turn out alright," I said more to myself more than him.

"So you do want to marry me, Mary?" He lowered his head, looking as if he expected me to reject him.

Taking my hand from his, I touched his chin and lifted his face. "Yes, I want to marry you."

I wasn't sure how all this was going to work out, but a peace settled somewhere inside of me. It wasn't huge, but it was enough to give me courage. Somehow, all of this was going to work out...it had to.

CHAPTER SEVEN

VACATION FROM WHAT

AFTER a day of convincing my father it was a great idea, my mother informed me that I could go to Elizabeth's house. I would be leaving in two days, and stay there until June, with enough time to help my dad before school began in August.

As elated as I was to be going, I had so many questions. I lay in bed at night wondering when everyone would be able to tell. I'd only seen a few movies about girls my age being pregnant, and most of the time it wasn't well received. I could only imagine with glimpses of horror, what my mother and father would say.

I tossed and turned until the wee hours of the morning, and finally gave up trying to go to sleep. My suitcase was stored somewhere in the garage, but I figured I could go ahead and fold up some stuff to put in it.

My closet wasn't very big, nor did I have a lot of clothing. Most of the stuff I'd had for years, but as I pulled it out, I was thankful it was all sort of big. Rubbing my stomach for the fiftieth time that night, I wondered what I would look like in three months. Some people didn't show at all for awhile, and it gave me some comfort to remember my mom saying she was one of them. Maybe it was genetic.

I came across my bathing suit and laughed. Even though it was a modest one-piece, I was quite sure I wouldn't get away with wearing it this summer. Tossing it back in the drawer, I came across something that Elizabeth had given me on my thirteenth birthday. It was an embroidered handkerchief with a saying on it.

"You are blessed when you believe," I read aloud. I held the cloth in my hand and raised my face toward the ceiling. "Oh, Creator," I whispered with my eyes closed. "I believe." Warmth spread over my body and I felt the tension ease. The wind blew outside, and I could hear the trees brushing against the side of the house.

Taking the handkerchief gingerly in my grasp, I laid it on my pillow. All my life I had believed every story my parents had told me about the Creator and the child that was to come. Never in a million years had I figured I'd be the mother of that child. Even though my mind was screaming how nuts all that sounded, I believed it. I kept the words of the angel in my heart, and no one could persuade me otherwise.

Soon I would have proof. The angel said Elizabeth was six months pregnant. There is no way that could be hidden, and something stirred within me as I thought about it. Only a miracle from the Creator could make something like that happen. I knew it was a sign for me. As soon as I saw Elizabeth, any unbelief would be driven completely away.

After a few hours, I heard the rest of my family getting up for the day. Although there was no point in me going to school, I wanted to turn in our science project. My mother had called Rebecca's mom, and Becs really had come down with the flu.

I hadn't spoken to her since the first night of my engagement, so after turning in our project, I planned to head over there to see her.

This morning there was no rain, but the streets and byways were sopping wet. I put on my boots and made my way through most of it fine. As I neared the school, the pit of my stomach felt funny. I was nervous to tell my teachers I was leaving for the rest of the year. They already thought my family was a bit odd, and I'm sure the engagement had reached their ears.

My mother had already called the office that morning to explain, so none of my teachers were shocked as I went around returning books. Some of them just smiled, while others showed their disgust openly, refusing to look me in the face. They didn't respond, when I said I'd see them next school year. No one seemed to believe me, and I realized after awhile, I didn't believe myself, when I said it. I had no idea if I'd be back at school in August or not. Depending on the timing of this baby, what stage of pregnancy would I be in? Would I even be allowed to go to school?

Dianna and Flower acted as if I told them I had cancer. I explained ten times why I wanted to go see my cousin, and finally they agreed it was a good idea. As I walked out the school doors, a sense of dread overwhelmed me. I had no idea how all this was going to be okay.

The walk to Rebecca's house was in the opposite direction of my house. Twenty minutes wasn't a long walk though, and if not for the mud, I would have made it sooner. The driveway to her house was long, so her mom saw me coming before I got all the way up to the house.

"Hey, Mary, darling!" She shouted. "You come on in, when

you get up here. Rebecca is in her room." The screen door swung shut as I continued my way up the drive.

Their front yard was so nice. Mrs. Levi had all sorts of statues and gardens planted. As soon as the season changed, if she wasn't at her job, she was out here planting and pruning.

I entered the house and went back to Rebecca's room. The curtains were open, and the television was on low.

"Hey, invalid," I teased her.

She coughed. "Hey, engaged lady." She smiled. "Let me see the ring."

I sat down on her bed and showed her my left hand. "What do you think?" I asked. "Kind of weird, huh?"

"Not weird," she responded and held my hand closer to her face. "It's a new perspective. I love the ring though. At least Joseph has good taste."

I smiled and took my hand from her. "Yeah."

"Do I detect the love bug has bitten, or are you glowing for no reason at all?' She asked readjusting herself on her pillows.

Self-conscious, I put my backpack on my lap in front of my stomach. "He's nice," I offered with a grin.

Rebecca laughed. "Okay, Mary, what are you not telling me?"

Smacking her playfully in the arm, I rolled my eyes. "I'm fifteen years old and engaged to be married. What's more important than that?"

She wasn't convinced. "Yeah, that would work if I hadn't known you for those last fifteen years. Spill it." She hit me back on the arm.

"Ow," I teased. "Alright." With a sigh I let her believe that the huge secret was coming. "I have decided to go stay with my cousin for the rest of the school year."

"What?" She asked sitting up in bed. "You're quitting school?"

"No, I'll be back in the fall." *I hope.*

"So what are you doing?"

I cleared my throat and explained. After ten minutes, Rebecca seemed to get why I wanted to go visit Elizabeth, but she was sad about it.

"I get it, but I won't get to see you for half the summer. And what about our science project? How in the world am I going to finish it alone?"

"Becs, would I leave you hanging?" I unzipped my back-pack and tossed her the logbook. "I went and checked out everything. All you have to do is take the plants into class. Mr. Prescott said just take pictures of the ones by the lake, and then you're done."

She yawned. "Wow, I guess you've got everything all figured out, huh?"

I shrugged. "Not everything." Waving my hand around with the ring on it, I smiled. "I'm sure there's quite a bit to figure out with this."

Rebecca took my hand in hers. "You'll do fine, Mary. My mom was talking about how amazing she thinks you and Joseph will be together. I think if he hadn't been taken with you, she would have tried to hook me up with him."

"Really?" I asked.

She laughed. " I don't know. It's just that she talks so much about the guy, I almost feel like I know him. Any ideas on when you two are tying the knot?"

I hadn't even thought about an exact day. Everyone kept saying it was written in our laws for me to remain with my parents for one more year after engagement. I hadn't thought about an exact date.

"Beats me," I finally replied. "I'm sure my mom will have it almost figured out by the time I get back."

"So...three months? Why so long?" She asked sadly.

"That's how long I always stay." I hugged her. "Don't be sad; I'll be back before you know it."

"Promise?"

Standing up I reached out and took her hand. "My father always says, 'let your yes be yes, and your no be no.' I can't promise exactly, but I will be back."

She looked disappointed, but smiled and blew me a kiss. I pretended to catch it and send her one right back.

"I love you, Mary," she said as I back up toward the door.

"I love you too, Rebecca."

I closed the door behind me and fought back the tears that were threatening to consume me. I hadn't lied to her, but I couldn't tell her the entire truth. The angel hadn't forbid me to tell anyone, but what exactly was I going to tell her? There weren't any words for what I was feeling. I needed to get to my cousin.

After dinner with my family, my father drug out the suit-case I would use for my journey. I didn't have much to take, and one bag would make it easier anyway. My backpack would come in handy for things I needed to get to quickly, and I felt more confident as the minutes ticked by.

Joseph had been away all day at a job, but promised to come by in the morning to take me to the bus station. My father and mother beamed with pride, when I told them that Joseph and I had talked about the marriage and everything was fine. I thanked them for their choice, and eagerly went to my room for the night.

I wasn't expecting to sleep, but I awoke suddenly at the sound of my mother's voice.

"Mary, dear, it's time to get ready to go. Joseph will be here soon."

I'd gone to bed in my sweatpants, so I just slipped on a hoodie and my shoes. After a quick brush and tie of my hair, I slipped on a ball cap and headed downstairs.

My mother had made me something to eat, and while we waited, my father appeared in his robe.

"You all ready, Mary?" He asked and hugged me.

"Yeah, dad."

"Tell Zachariah we appreciate him letting you come stay. I'm sure Elizabeth's been wanting you to come anyway.'"

"Yes," my mother agreed. "Beth always adored you, Mary. No matter how far apart you two ever were, there was always some special connection."

I sighed. "I can't wait to see them." *I really couldn't wait to see her.*

Someone knocked on the kitchen door. I was expecting Joseph, but the anticipation of seeing his face was unexpected.

"Hey, Joe!" My father greeted him and walked to shake his hand.

"Good morning. I trust we're all having a blessed break-fast," he responded with a hint in his voice.

My mother laughed. "There's plenty, Joseph. Have a seat."

The four of us sat around the table and talked. My dad was giving last minute instructions about my commitment to be back by June, and my mother actually talked about the wedding. Both subjects made me want to run screaming. By June, things would either be really special, or really terrible.

After fifteen minutes, I went into Amber and Colin's rooms to say goodbye to each of them. Colin barely acknowledged me, but Amber was actually awake.

"Hey, silly," I teased her. "Why didn't you come eat with us?"

She shrugged. "Whatever."

I stepped closer to her and could see tears on her face. "Amber?"

She embraced me. "I'm going to miss you, Mary."

"It's okay, Amber. I'll be back in three months. We'll go get ice cream my first day back. By June, Frosty Freeze will be open."

"I know." She sniffled and laughed. "And don't tell anyone I cried. I've got to keep up my reputation."

I laughed. "No problem. I'll call you from the phone in town."

Instead of answering she threw her pillow at me. I turned the light back out and went to the kitchen. Joseph was standing with my suitcase in hand. My mother usually smiled, when I was on my way to Elizabeth's, but today she looked sad.

"I'll be fine, mom," I said, giving her a huge hug.

"I know, sweetheart. I'm just going to miss you is all."

My dad came up behind me. "Give me one for the road too, Mary."

I hugged him and then looked at them both. "I love you... so much. I'll call when I get there."

Joseph went out the door and down the steps. I followed him quietly. Trying to swallow the big lump in my throat, I didn't want to start crying in the house. My mom was already welled up as I turned away, and I had to have more courage than I'd ever had in my life. From this moment forward I was embracing the unknown. Rubbing my hand on my belly, I realized the unknown was inevitable. An angel had shown up and told me I was the mother of the Son of the Creator. My predicament defined the word 'unknown.'

My bus didn't leave for another forty-five minutes, so I didn't mind how slow Joseph seemed to drive. I was so nervous I didn't notice that I had started shaking.

His voice was kind as he spoke. "Are you cold, Mary? I can turn the heater on for you."

Squeezing my hands open and shut, I turned to him. "No, I'm not cold. Just a little nervous," I admitted.

Joseph reached over and took my little hand in his. This was the third time he'd ever even touched me. The action instantly calmed me, and I grasp gently onto his fingers.

"Everything's going to go smoothly. Just think, in a few months you'll be back and the harvest will be going on. And this fall you'll get to be part of the women's ceremonies for the festival."

I hadn't thought about that. During the fall, we had festivals, where the engaged or married women performed dances to celebrate the feast. I'd been taught the dances for the last few years in preparation. It was a very proud moment for families, when their daughters were eligible to dance.

At my silence, Joseph squeezed my hand and continued. "And then the winter snows will come. I get to stop work for about two months and we'll have more time to hang out...get to know each other more." He smiled. I actually really liked his smile.

We pulled up in front of the bus terminal. I wanted to stay

inside the warmth of the truck, but just beyond those doors was the gateway to my new reality.

"Thank you, Joseph," I said looking over at him.

He rubbed my hand softly. "You're welcome, Mary. I'll be looking forward to your return."

Letting go of my hand, he pulled into a parking space. I hopped out as he got my bag. After checking it in for the right bus, I turned to him with a sigh.

"Well, I guess this is it," I offered. "Hopefully we'll see each other in three months."

"Hopefully?" He asked with a grin. "I'd say, may the Creator bless you until we see each other again. May He bless it to be in three months or sooner."

This time Joseph came closer and hugged me. The smell of his jacket lingered as he pulled slightly away. I couldn't look up right now; if I did I'd cry. Joseph was my last thread to hold onto, but I had to let go.

"Bye," I whispered and turned. I didn't look behind me. I knew he was there watching me walk away, but I couldn't bear it. I had no idea if the man behind me would even want to look at me when I returned.

CHAPTER EIGHT

ARTIFICIAL INSEMINATION

WE stopped a few times along the way, but for the most part, my journey consisted of seeing the back of the seat in front of me. I stretched when we stopped, but never really found myself too comfortable.

Just when I was resigned to my riding torture, I heard the driver's voice announce we had reached our destination. I looked out the window relieved. It was ten o'clock in the morning, and people were busy on the streets. I wasn't sure what time we'd get here, and I was glad it was so early in the morning. My cousins tended to go to bed early in the evening, so this way I was sure to catch them up and around.

I was glad they lived on the outskirts of town. No big city hassle to go through, I retrieved my bag and headed over to the bus counter.

"Excuse me, ma'am," I asked the lady on the other side of the ticket counter.

"Yes, young lady," she answered with a smile.

"I was needing a ride out to my cousin's farm. Do you know the best way for me to do that?"

She thought for a moment. "I'd head over to the grocery store. It's just a block over from here to the north. Farmers are always picking up supplies in the morning. Someone should be able to give you a ride."

"Thank you," I said and made my way out the station.

Following her directions, I crossed the street and walked the short distance. The grocery store was full of people, and I saw a familiar face.

"Ms. Anna!" I yelled over the noise.

Her curly hair bobbed around the customers in front of her and she laughed.

"Well, if it isn't my Mary! What are you doing here girl?"

I set my backpack on the counter. "I've come to visit Elizabeth and Zachariah."

"Oh, how lovely. I haven't seen her come to town for the last couple of months. Zachariah hasn't been in longer than that. They must have had a hard winter. Those ranch hands of theirs have been doing most of the shopping. There's Ezra now."

I turned to see a guy not much older than me.

"Ezra!" Anna shouted. The boy turned her direction. "Come here!"

He made his way up to the counter. "Yeah."

She pointed to me. "This here is Mary. Mary, this is Ezra."

"Hello," I said and waved at him.

"Hey," he replied.

Anna reached over and produced some envelopes. "Here, Mary. You take these to your kin. I've had 'em here behind the desk for near a month. Ezra," she said and turned to him. "Tell your father Mary needs a ride to Zachariah's place."

"Alright," he answered and smiled at me.

She reached out and touched my hand. "Good to see you again, girl. Give them my best."

"Of course," I replied and turned toward Ezra.

"Where's your truck or whatever?" I asked and pulled my suitcase.

"It's out back. Here, let me get that," he offered.

"No." I shook my head. "I've got it, thanks." I felt it was important to be as independent as possible.

"Okay then," he responded with a smirk. "Just follow me."

We made our way through the crowd to the back of the store. Squeezing past pallets of flour and salt, I forced my suitcase through to the door. A huge farm truck was there already running.

"Where ya been?" A man's voice asked. I looked over to see an older man walking up to the driver's side door.

"Anna asked us to give her a ride," Ezra replied not saying my name.

"I'm Mary," I said extending my hand to shake his. "I'm a cousin of Elizabeth and Zachariah."

The man squinted at me in disbelief. "You're a cousin of Ole' Zach?"

I laughed. "Actually, Elizabeth is my cousin by blood, but yes."

He shook his head. "Well, I'm Nehemiah, most folks call me Ned. How long you here for?" He asked taking my suitcase.

"For about three months. I was here last summer, but I don't remember you." I followed him to the back of the pick-up.

Ned let the tailgate down and tossed up my bag. He then extended his hand to help me up.

"We just joined on there this year. The last two fellas they had got their own land just East of here. Be careful," he added as I hopped up on the back.

"Oh, Mr. March left?"

"Sure did. Just about the time your cousin lost his voice I figure." He slammed the tailgate shut.

"Lost his voice?" I asked as he rounded the side of the truck.

Ned nodded. "Yeah. He just stopped talking one day. We all figured it was just something to do with his age and all. He hasn't said much about it," he said with a wink.

The ride to the farm was about thirty minutes. The back of the truck wasn't too comfortable, but I knew they'd put me back here. This way I wouldn't be seen alone in a truck with two men. As old fashioned as it seemed, the reputation of a girl could be tainted over the simplest thing.

I placed my hand over my stomach and thought about the baby. I wasn't even sure I was pregnant yet. The angel said I would conceive a son, but not exactly when. Elizabeth being pregnant had something to do with the timing though. I wonder what she would say, if I told her. Out of everyone in my family though, I felt she would be the most understanding no matter what happened.

Sleeping well on the bus hadn't been much of an option. I didn't feel comfortable around strangers, so I had barely slept. As we rode to the farm, I lied down and put my backpack beneath my head.

The clouds above me were so beautiful. They looked like they were being blown free by the wind. My life had gone beyond complicated; I was officially in a moment of chaos. I held my hand up in the sunlight. My ring sparkled rainbows onto the sides of the truck. Joseph. I wonder what he was doing right now.

The truck swerved heavily tossing me over to my side. We went from being on asphalt to a very bumpy road, so I decided to sit up. Familiar landscape greeted me, and my heart pulsed with anticipation. I could see the outline of the main house, and my world was about to change. Elizabeth was either going to be six months pregnant, or I was going to be very confused.

Dusting off my sleeve, I adjusted my ball cap and tried to remain calm. We slowed down, and I closed my eyes. Within the next minute, I would come face to face with reality. Elizabeth had to be pregnant; the angel said she was. When I saw she was pregnant, that would mean I would be too.

"You need a hand out?" Ned asked.

I opened my eyes and reached for his hand. A moment later, I was on the ground, but my feet felt unstable. I felt like I would fall over or run screaming from anxiety. I heard a loud banging noise, and recognized the familiar slam of Elizabeth's screen door.

Ned had taken my suitcase up to the front porch, and I walked alongside the truck, bracing myself for the sight of her. As I neared the front of the truck, I took a deep breath and looked over. It wasn't her.

Ezra walked over to me. "Ms. Beth is probably out back with the chickens. She usually is this time of morning."

"Thanks," I said and exhaled. Shaking my head I walked toward the side of the house. Before I knew it I was running and calling her name.

"Elizabeth! Elizabeth!" I yelled rounding the corner.

I saw a woman bent down near the ground about fifty yards away. When I yelled, she stood up, but paused and didn't directly turn around. The closer I got, I could tell it was her. My heart accelerated and I ran with all that was in me toward her.

She turned, hand on her protruding stomach, and looked at me shocked. A moment later, her wide smile greeted me and I was in her arms.

"Blessed are you of all the women on earth, Mary! Blessed is the child within you!"

We stopped spinning and she grabbed my face looking deep within my eyes. Tears fell freely from within my spirit to my eyes, and I couldn't stop crying.

She smiled. "How in the world has this happened to me, that the mother of my Lord should come visit me?"

"Beth," I sobbed. How did you know?"

"When you said my name, my baby jumped around as if for joy. You are so blessed, Mary, that you believed what the angel from our Creator told you."

The roundness of Elizabeth's stomach stuck out far enough to touch me. I looked down hesitantly, but she took my hand and placed it on her belly. I was rewarded with a resounding thump from inside of her, and I cried even harder.

"It's true," I told her through my sobs. "It's all true. You're pregnant."

She laughed. "Yes, honey. This old lady is actually pregnant. Took us all by a surprise, but Zachariah was told first. He didn't believe it though...well, I'll explain all that later." She hugged me again. "Now," she said letting me go. "Come inside, your Zach will be anxious to see you. We had no idea it would be you, of course."

Elizabeth waddled along beside me. It was so weird to see her pregnant at such an old age. Every other step I almost wanted to catch her from being off-balance.

"Hey, Beth," I said as we neared the house.

"Yes, honey."

"An angel told me you were six months pregnant."

She patted my hand. "And he was right. I'm six months since last week."

Opening the back door of the house, I let her go through first. The room was light enough from the sunlight, and I immediately saw my cousin Zachariah.

"Look who's here," Elizabeth exclaimed.

At the sound of her voice, Zachariah looked up from the paper he was reading. His face looked so worn; older than the last time I had seen him. But a smile in the wrinkle of his eyes widened, when he looked over at Elizabeth. He then looked back at me and stood up.

"Hey, Zachariah," I said and walked toward him.

He embraced me in a huge hug, lifting me almost off the floor. For a guy near seventy, he was very strong.

Elizabeth tapped me on the arm. "He's lost his voice, so he'll write you something." She nodded toward a table next to his chair. On it were piles of paper and a pen.

Zachariah let me go and sat down. Furiously he began to write. I walked over to the couch by the window and sat down. Their house smelled so good. I'd come out here for the last three summers, but they had lived here for over ten years. Zachariah had inherited the property from his parents, and he and Elizabeth had moved when I was five years old.

After a moment, he stood up excitedly and handed me a couple of pages.

My dear Mary,

How excited are we that you have come to visit us. As you can see and hear, I have no voice. It is only my fault that this has occurred. An angel of the Creator came to me six months ago. He told me that Elizabeth was to bear a child, a child that would be the forerunner of the Creator's Son born in flesh.

He said that Elizabeth would bear a son, and we were to call him John. He would be kindred to the Son of the Creator, but I had no idea that it would be you. When you walked into the room today, it astounded me that you were the virgin of the prophecies from long ago.

I didn't believe the words of the angel, and for my disbelief I have lost my voice. I have made peace with the Creator on this, and am humbled that he has allowed my family to play this part in His will. Bless you, Mary. You will be called blessed for all of time. Bless you. I love you.

Tears splashed off my face onto the paper. It shook in my hands, as I trembled with the reality of what had just been told to me. I felt sick. The room felt way too hot, and I had to stand up and take off my hoodie.

Dropping the paper on the couch beside me, I stood and pulled the hoodie over my head. My ball cap came off in the process, and the room felt like it was spinning. I felt my stomach gurgle and knew what was eminent.

Dashing through the living room, I headed to the closest bathroom. Just in time, I made it to the toilet and vomited. When I thought it had past, I stood straight up, but another wave of nausea hit me...hard.

I knelt down in front of the toilet, clinging to it like a life-preserve. My stomach wretched in and out, over and over again, and I felt like I couldn't catch my breath. Something cool was touched to the back of my neck, and I heard Elizabeth's voice.

"It has begun," she whispered sweetly. "You'll be okay, honey. It's like this in the early stages."

"Early stages of what?" I asked wiping my mouth.

She laughed. "Pregnancy."

A wave of nausea hit me again, so I didn't have time to respond. At one point my head felt hot and spinning, so I actually lay it on the toilet seat. I heard Elizabeth's kind voice from time to time, how in the world was I going to get through this?

I'm not sure how long I was in the bathroom, but eventually Elizabeth walked me to the extra room and I lay down. A cold cloth was placed on my head, and I felt better and better as the moments ticked by.

A loud ringing sound clanged outside, and I knew it was noon. They still held fast to the tradition of calling everyone to eat by the large triangle on the front porch. I couldn't even imagine eating food, but I didn't want to lie in this room alone too much longer.

I laughed. "But I guess I'm not alone," I whispered aloud rubbing my stomach. I guess the question of when it would happen was answered. I was pregnant. This was insemination on a whole new level. I hadn't felt a thing. If I hadn't just thrown up my entire stomach contents, I wouldn't have even had any idea. I wonder when it happened?

"Mary, honey, are you feeling better?" Elizabeth's soft voice rescued me from going into a panic.

I nodded. "Yeah," I said sitting up. "I feel better."

"Well, if you think your stomach can handle it, you may want to try to eat a little something. I found it actually helped with the nausea. When's the last time you ate?" She brushed my hair out of my face with her hand.

"Hmm, let's see. I don't think I even ate breakfast."

"Ah, that's why. We'll just try to get you some bread and water for starters."

Laughing, I stood up. "You just offered me prison food, Beth."

"Well," she smiled. "I guess I did. But it is awful good bread. We make it from our own wheat."

She took my arm and we began to walk. I couldn't help but look down at her stomach. I wasn't sure what was normal and what wasn't, but Elizabeth's stomach looked huge to me.

"Beth?" I asked and she looked up.

"Yes."

"Does it...hurt?" I winced as I asked the question.

"This?" She asked pointing to her stomach. She shook her head. "No, this isn't that part that I imagined would hurt. Now in about three months, labor might be a bit of an issue."

I felt my face get flush. "Wow, you mean I'll be here for the birth?"

She thought for a moment as we entered the kitchen. "Well, I guess you will be, honey. Isn't it wonderful how the Creator works things out?"

Ned, Ezra and my uncle were all seated at the table. When we entered, they all stood, and we sat down at our places. Ezra looked at me and smiled, then handed me the basket of bread.

"Here you go, Mary," he said and smiled. "Ms. Beth said you were sick. Are you okay now?"

I nodded. "Yeah."

"Well, it's probably just all the riding you've done today. My dad can be a reckless driver with that truck." He looked over at his dad.

Ned looked at him over a pair of glasses. "I've been driving that truck since before you were born, boy. My driving has never been suspect to reckless."

Everyone laughed. Zachariah smiled, and continued to eat. I noticed he had a piece of paper and a pen at the table.

"So, Mary," Elizabeth began. "You mentioned being here for three months?"

"Yes," I replied and sipped some water. "I'll need to be back home by June. Dad needs me to help with the mill this year."

"Oh, I see. So how is school? You graduate in two years?"

My silence was so long, I even felt awkward. I had so many rapid thoughts shooting around my head, and Elizabeth seemed to realize her question was a bit loaded.

She patted my hand. "I suppose the future will take care of itself." Elizabeth looked around the table. "Ned and Ezra have been with us for a few months, but we've known Ned for years. I was one of the women who helped Ezra's mom bring his little brother into this world," she said with pride. "Not many babies born around here the last ten years that I didn't have a hand on."

Ezra laughed. "My mom nearly fell over, when Ms. Elizabeth told us all she was having a baby."

"That she did," Ned chimed in. "It's a blessing from the Creator for sure. Zachariah has been such a faithful keeper of the prophecies. It didn't surprise me at all that he and Beth would somehow be part of them."

I smiled at the loving look that my cousins exchanged one to the other. It really was an honor that the Creator had chosen my family to unfold His will for mankind.

"Mary!" Elizabeth exclaimed so loudly I jumped.

"What? What is it?" I thought maybe something was up with her baby.

"The ring!" She exclaimed. "You're wearing a ring on your wedding finger?" She looked very confused.

"Oh," I said. Sighing I turned the ring around on my finger. "Dad and mom chose someone for me to marry last week. I'm engaged."

Elizabeth immediately expressed the weight of my announcement.

"Oh my, child. Is he a believer? Does he know of things to come?" She asked in a way, I knew she hadn't told Ned or Ezra.

I shook my head. "He believes in the prophecies of our Creator, but he expects that I will return alone in June." I could tell by her eyes that she understood that Joseph had no idea that I was pregnant.

She sighed. "We will pray. We will pray these three months for a word from our Lord. Surely he will not leave you to deal with such things." Elizabeth patted my hand. "Now, eat. We will let tomorrow take care of itself. Today, we are rejoicing in the arrival of our beautiful cousin. To cousin Mary." She lifted her glass.

Everyone in the room followed suit, and Zachariah smiled wider and nodded his head with his glass raised. I wasn't sure how the next three months were going to end, but I felt safe here. Elizabeth was pregnant...and so was I.

CHAPTER NINE

SETTLING IN

THE first month of my visit was pretty much like the first day. I ate food, and then I threw up food. I slept more than I ever had in my life, and apologized daily for falling asleep mid-conversation.

Ezra's older sister, Esther, had come by after a few days. Elizabeth had really started to slow down, now in her seventh month, so Esther began to check on us both daily. No one asked any questions about why I was so sick, but Esther seemed to pick up on my 'issue.' I was mortified the day she asked me about it.

"So," Esther said, smiling over a basket of seeds. "How long have you been married?"

I'm sure the shocked look on my face told her more than my answer.

"Uh...I've had the ring for a month."

"Oh," she responded, apparently receiving my answer as a good one. "You know, it happens sometimes."

"What?" I asked before thinking about what she was referring to.

Esther nodded at my stomach. "Babies. There have been other couples that have had babies before their ceremony.

In days past, the engagement actually meant that they were married. The year waiting period is just to prove chastity."

If I hadn't just thrown up, I probably would have. I didn't have an explanation that would suffice, so I changed the subject and asked her about which seeds to plant. Later that night I lay awake wondering if that's what everyone would assume. Joseph of course would know we never hooked up, and if he told everyone that, they would assume the worst.

My reputation was the last thing I was concerned about at the moment. I was daily shocked and overwhelmed by the fact that I was pregnant. I was going to be someone's mother, and not just anyone. The Creator had decided to come as a Son to this world, and He had promised long ago to help restore balance.

We lived by so many laws, and it was told that after the Creator came, we would be able to be redeemed though sinful. I wasn't sure what all of it meant, but I had believed the prophecy even as a little child.

My mother and father made it a point to teach us. From the age of three on, I learned to recite verses from their stories. It was too dangerous to write them down, so we learned them and kept them in our hearts.

Every day here, I'd take my prayer shawl and kneel toward the East. I'd ask the Creator to bless my body to fulfill the task He had designed, and though I was frightened of the unknown with this pregnancy, I had peace knowing His will was being done.

I had called my parents a few days after I arrived. My mother cried, and said how proud she was of me for being so mature about the wedding situation. She informed me that she had seen the foundation of the house Joseph was building, and that it promised to be a nice place to start a family. Her choice of words couldn't have been more prophetic.

The second month of my pregnancy ended toward the end of May, and for what I lacked in size, Elizabeth doubled. There were times that Zachariah and I both watched with worry, but she was strong. She said the Creator had not only given her a son, but He had restored her youth to bear him.

Nausea had stopped plaguing me so much, and I found myself settling in to the idea of having a baby. There were still no outward signs, but I noticed at night when I'd go to bed that I felt different. The only way to explain it was I didn't ever feel alone. Even if no one was within a mile of me, I had an overwhelming sense of not being by myself.

Elizabeth was going to bed earlier and earlier at night, so Ezra, Esther and I started spending more time together. We'd go for long walks in the evening, always sure to return before it got too late. I had so much fun with them, swimming, hiking, and for the most part enjoying my time.

There weren't many people that lived in the area, and rural people usually didn't have many visits from the soldiers. In many ways, I felt safer here with the baby, than I would at home. I knew this visit had worked out at the right timing. If I had been at home, the vomiting would have been an immediate cause for intervention by my mom. I imagine she would have taken me to the doctor, and that would have been a hard thing to explain.

On one of our evening walks, Ezra asked me the strangest question.

"So, Mary?"

"Yeah," I responded while picking up a stone.

"Esther says you're knocked up."

I looked over at Esther. She looked the other way. "Well, Esther would be correct," I answered him, while still looking at her.

He continued. "I'm not being weird or anything, I just wondered is all." Ezra ended his sentence a little sheepishly.

"I'm engaged to a guy back home. His name is Joseph. I'll be married by this time next year." I didn't know what else to say.

He looked disappointed. "If he's going to marry you, then why did your parents send you way out here?"

I stopped walking and turned fully toward him. "My parents didn't send me here, exactly," I admitted. Sighing I walked a little faster, but he caught up.

"I wasn't trying to be funny, Mary." He looked back behind us at Esther. She slowed her steps. "Esther told me you were pregnant, because I asked her why you were here. I couldn't understand someone engaged being away from their fiancé, unless there was something weird going on."

Tears formed in my eyes. "So you decided to ask. I suppose just for the sake of knowing?" I started to walk.

He walked beside me. "No….well, yes, but not just to know. I just wondered if he still wanted to be with you. Because… because if he didn't want you because of the baby, well, I don't mind it at all."

I stopped walking again and shook my head. "Ezra, you have no idea what you are saying. It's sweet, but you have no idea."

Ezra reached out and took my hand. "I know I don't have much, and I'm only eighteen, but I'm a hard worker. Mary, I really have taken a liking to you these past two months. You're sweet." He raised his hand as if to touch my face. Out of nowhere, lightning flashed and thunder rippled across the sky. Furious raindrops fell, and the wind picked up instantly.

The wind said my name, and a familiar anxiety rippled up my spine. I removed my hand from his and took a step back.

"I better get home!" I yelled above the elements. "I'll see you guys tomorrow."

Turning abruptly, I ran with all my might toward the house. I felt a weight on my shoulders, even though I knew I had done nothing wrong. Ezra was a nice guy, and it must have taken a lot for him to say the things he did.

I ran in the house with water dripping off me from head to toe. Zachariah looked at me questioningly, then got up and came back with a towel. He smiled, and nodded toward the bedroom so I'd know Elizabeth was asleep.

"Thank you," I whispered, so as not to wake her, and headed back toward the spare room. After removing my wet clothes, I sat on my bed brushing my hair. I cried, but it wasn't overwhelming, I just felt sad. I could only hope that Joseph's response would be even close to Ezra's.

Late into the night I sat there. I couldn't sleep, so I went to the kitchen for a snack. My cousins didn't have much junk food here, but I loved the pickles that they kept in stock. Quietly opening the jar, I took out a pickle and then put the jar back. I looked out the back screen door. Living so far out in the country, one didn't have to worry about locking everything up.

I stepped out on the porch and the coolness of the night washed over me. I breathed deep and exhaled, wondering just how the Creator had looked down and chosen me. Of all the young women in the world, He had designed me to bear His essence. I lay my hand on my stomach as I savored my pickle.

"Mary?" Elizabeth's soft voice stirred me.

"Yeah, Beth." I turned to see her waddling out the door.

"You can't sleep, child?"

I shook my head. "No." I laughed. "Had to have a pickle." I raised my hand to show her.

"Oh, my." She joined me laughing. "I remember those days. There was a time I'd flat out cry if there were none left. Zachariah remembered, and makes sure the boys always bring them back for you from town."

"I didn't know that," I said with a smile. "How considerate of him."

She put her arm around my waist. "It is truly our honor, Mary. To be blessed with our own son is one thing; but to be blessed to witness the onset of the Holy One is...well, it's just such a blessing."

Hugging her back, I held my pickle to the side. "You are a blessing, Beth. All my life I've had so much love from you. You always encouraged me, and believed in me, even when I couldn't believe in myself."

We stood there for a few moments looking up at the moon. The wind blew gently, as if caressing our faces as we stood looking out. I must have seen the moon hundreds of times, but tonight for some reason, it looked even more beautiful. Somewhere up there, the Creator was looking down on us. I could only hope He was pleased.

Elizabeth sighed. "Well, I better be getting back to bed. If I stand too long, my ankles seem to swell."

"Of course," I said and opened the door for her. "I'll be in shortly."

"Rest easy, Mary. All will be well." She patted my arm as she walked past me into the house.

I let the screen door shut quietly behind her and decided to sit down on the porch swing. The night air felt crisp and light, and I could stay out here forever. I lay my head against the back of the chair and looked up at the moon. I wondered what my family was doing right now. It was about two hours in time difference, so they should all be sleeping.

My ring glistened in the light of the moon. With no city lights to dim the natural light, everything had a beautiful blue hue to it. It looked beautiful, and I twisted it around and around.

A coyote bellowed a loud cry from somewhere in the darkness. It sent chills down my spine, and I felt more alive than I had in the past couple of months. After finishing my pickle I went back inside the house. I lay down feeling like the world was so much bigger than I had thought before.

* * * * * *

It was nearing the end of June. I managed to have grown a tiny belly bump, and sometimes I stayed in the mirror for half an hour trying to see any change at all. The nausea had finally left all together, but my appetite had increased. Elizabeth and Zachariah laughed at how much I could eat in a setting, and Zachariah wrote me little notes teasing me from time to time.

Poor Elizabeth looked like she would pop at any moment. She spent more time sitting, knitting little things for the son that would soon be here. Some ladies from town had actually stopped by, completely shocked and elated about her pregnancy.

When I asked her why she hadn't said anything, her answer was not what I expected.

"Hey, Beth. Why didn't you let anyone know about your baby?" I asked her while we were folding clothes.

She squinted her eyebrows for a moment and then put

down the shirt she was folding. "Well, at first I was so shocked, it didn't cross my mind. Then when I thought about it, I knew it was something that Zachariah would have loved to tell the congregation. When he could no longer speak, we stopped having the weekly meetings. I didn't want to take that away from him."

"Oh, wow," I said. "I hadn't even thought about that. Do you think he'll get his voice back?"

"I think so. I believe our Creator understands when we struggle with doubt. Zachariah has served the Lord his entire life. I think in the end, our Father will bless him with his voice." At the end of her sentence she made a really weird face. It wasn't pain exactly, but it didn't look comfortable.

"Are you okay?" I asked and walked over to her.

"Yeah," she said through clinched teeth. These pains come and go this past week. The time is surely nearing." She smiled, but I could see she was really uncomfortable.

"How will you know when it's time?" I asked rubbing her shoulder.

"You know, I'm not sure." The tension in her face lessened. "I've helped deliver many babies over the years. Most mothers say they just know." She smiled and took my hand. "Mary, can you believe the time is so close?"

Squeezing her hand, I sat down on the couch by her. "Are you ever...afraid?" I swallowed hard.

Elizabeth paused for a moment, reached up and brushed my hair from my face. "There is an element of anxiety about the unknown, but I don't think our Father wants us to be afraid. He has done such a miraculous thing, and I have to believe that all will turn out right." She raised my chin up higher. "Do not be afraid of what man could ever do to you, child. You are the mother of the Son; the One who has been sent to free us all from the rulers that have treated us so poorly."

A sudden knock on the door made us both jump. I stood up and went to answer. On the porch was a man dressed head to toe in military fatigues. The screen door was between us, but I felt as if my space was seriously invaded.

"Zachariah Miller," he said staunchly.

I nodded and turned to see my cousin Zachariah coming up beside me. He nodded at the man and stepped in front of me.

"Are you Zachariah Miller?" He asked looking at my cousin.

Zachariah nodded again, and looked over his shoulder at me.

"He's unable to talk," I explained.

The man looked annoyed. "Well, can he hear?" He asked bluntly.

Once again my cousin nodded at the man.

Opening a piece of paper, the man began to read. "It is hereby announced on this day, that you must pay a fine for the misuse of the waterway. Pay the fine within ten days, and your land will not be taken as penalty." With that said, the man extended the piece of paper.

Zachariah nodded as he opened the screen door and took the paper. The solider immediately turned and walked off the porch to his waiting vehicle.

Zachariah crumbled the paper in his hand and rushed back toward their room. Elizabeth had gotten up off the couch, though she hadn't quite made it to the door where we were.

She looked concerned. "Is everything alright?" She asked with her hand bracing her back.

I shrugged. "The man said something about a fine about the waterway."

Elizabeth rolled her eyes. "Every year they make up that lame fine. The water is on our land and runs off onto some property the government bought. Beavers dam up the site every year, and they fine us for it; as if we could control the animals." She sighed. "I better go see how Zachariah is doing. He tends to get real upset at this stuff."

I turned to watch the man drive off in his jeep and shuddered. I wondered what he would have done if he'd known about the child I carried within me. Protectively I laid my hand on my belly, instantly what felt like bubbles moved.

Gasping, I pressed my hand firmer against my shirt. It happened again. "Beth!" I yelled sprinting toward the back of the house."

She was sitting on their bed next to Zachariah. They both looked up in alarm.

"What is it, Mary?" She asked.

"It moved!" I said loudly.

Zachariah shrugged at me, and Elizabeth asked, "What moved, dear?"

Walking up beside her, I leaned down and grabbed her hand putting it to my stomach.

"The baby...he moved."

Tears brimmed my eyes. Elizabeth began to cry, and Zachariah knelt beside their bed, obviously praying. What joy I felt in my soul. I couldn't imagine a more precious moment than this. The Son of the Creator, moved beneath my skin. He felt so alive and a part of me, but I knew I only housed the Divine. At that moment I knew. Whatever befell me at the hands of men because of this pregnancy, it was worth it. My only mission now was to bring Him into the world...alive.

CHAPTER TEN

CHANGE IS PERMANENT

A loud noise woke me up in the middle of night. I rolled over to see Zachariah coming through the door of my room. His hand motions flailed rapidly, and I got up as quick as I could to follow him.

I was surprised to see other women in the room, and Esther was by my side.

"It's time, Mary," she explained and patted me on the back. I looked from her face to the living room entrance, and a loud scream pierced my ears. I pushed past Zachariah and saw Elizabeth with Esther's mom and another woman on the floor. The table had been moved out the way, and a dim light was burning.

"Get me more ice," Esther's mom told her.

For some reason I stood half shocked. I couldn't believe this was already happening. The birth of Elizabeth's son brought such finality to the situation. From this moment on, so to speak, there was no turning back.

Another yell rippled across the room sending tingles up my spine. I looked over at Esther's mom. "What can I do?" I asked.

Despite the situation she smiled calmly. "Not much to do but wait, sweetie."

Elizabeth reached out for my hand. I wanted to move forward and take it, but for some reason my feet wouldn't move. This was all just too overwhelming.

"Mary," she whispered. "Mary, do not be afraid."

Tears formed in my eyes, but I refused to succumb to them. With all my will I made myself move toward her. Kneeling down I took her hand. It was hot and shaky.

"Are you okay?" I asked, realizing it was probably a stupid question.

She nodded, but a distorted expression overtook her face. A second later she moaned in a manner that I'd never heard before, squeezing my hand so hard it hurt. A prayer left my heart for the Creator to help her through this.

We sat there like that for hours. Just as sunlight began to drip like rain through the curtain, the cry of a newborn baby echoed throughout the house. John was here. The miracle baby promised nine months ago by the Creator was here.

I felt a bubbly feeling within me, and I knew it was a sign of joy. I watched Elizabeth with her newborn son and knew that the time had come for me to leave. Baby John's birth signaled the beginning of a new chapter in my life.

The women cleaned up little John and helped Elizabeth return to her bed. I stayed by her side, gazing at the new baby. As tired as she was, Elizabeth looked even younger and full of complete peace. She rocked her new son slowly back and forth, while singing a song of thanksgiving for what the Creator had done.

Exhausted, I forced myself to leave her to get some rest. I curled up under my covers, wrapping my arms around my stomach. The Son I carried would one day be born into this world. How was it that I was so blessed? This child would one day change the government and bring order to all of mankind.

The next two days were absolute bliss. I had never seen Elizabeth smile so much, and Zachariah all but danced around twenty-four hours a day. He sat beside Elizabeth writing so much, we joked that he was writing a book.

As I began folding my clothing to be packed, I was thankful that my stomach really hadn't changed. At three months pregnant, it looked like I had just eaten too much at Thanksgiving dinner. I could feel what I called 'baby bubbles' from time to time, but it was still a rare occasion.

In three days I would be home. I had talked to my parents on the phone twice a month since being here, and it freaked me out the closer it got to June. Just last week I had told them I was fine, and how I was looking forward to returning home. Now I stood wondering if they'd even allow me to stay in their home, once they found out I was pregnant.

Ever since the day in the greenhouse, I wondered if the angel would return with any more instructions. He had only told me of the events to come, but not anything on how to handle it with my family. And even if my family wound up believing me, what would happen in our community? Half the people I knew would probably never speak to me again.

"What are you so intense about?" Esther's voice startled me.

I turned to see her leaning against the doorframe of my room. She looked so at ease about everything. She had been married once, but her husband had died in a trailer accident. At twenty-six years of age, she was a widow, with no children, and talked about one day getting remarried.

"Just thinking about home," I admitted and sat down on my bed.

She walked toward me. "Don't sweat it, Mary. As old fashioned as our people can be, times have changed. Your engagement was a public deal before the pregnancy; besides, you really can't even tell you're knocked up." She laughed trying to make me feel better.

"But that can't last forever," I said rubbing my stomach. "I figure in another month I'll be forced to explain."

Esther shrugged. "What's there to explain? As long as that Joseph guy says the baby is his, no one is going to care." She walked over and patted me on the arm. "It's going to be okay, Mary. The only one who will be upset for a little while is Ezra." She winked at me.

I had felt so bad about that. After his declaration of affection for me that night, I'd hardly seen him. When they would come over for dinner he tried to be normal, but it was never the same.

"Is he alright?" I asked with genuine concern.

With a smile she began to fold one of my shirts. "He'll be fine, Mary. You're just the first person he ever really had a crush on. When he doesn't have to run into you every day, I think his heart will mend." Esther walked over to the window. "It's so hot outside now."

I stood and walked over. "I know. Back home it's even hotter."

"That's going to make your baby bump hard to hide soon, huh? No more hoodies."

Looking down I smoothed my shirt down. "Like I said." I sighed. "In about a month, I think I'll have some explaining to do."

Esther reached over and hugged me. "It will be alright, girl. You are one of the most amazing people I've ever met. People who truly love you and know you won't be too taken aback. Sometimes people make mistakes and things happen."

At the mention of the word 'mistake,' my stomach churned. My baby wasn't a mistake. He was my destiny. I walked back over to my bed, a sudden sadness engulfing me. Of course everyone would assume the way Esther had, but then what would Joseph assume? Was it fair for me to let anyone assume it was his baby? Was it even right?

The rest of the night I packed and straightened out everything in the room. I made sure to spend time holding the baby, a new accomplishment I'd achieved within the last day. Elizabeth made sure I held him, and even wanted me to help give him his first real bath. It was mind blowing to know that in six short months, I would be doing the same thing with my own son.

It was weird in a way to think of Him as my son. I mean, yes, He was growing inside of me and I would give birth to Him, but He wasn't really a part of me. The only DNA He had belonged to the Creator, and I was just like those surrogate moms I'd seen on television.

The Son was promised to be the Creator in the flesh; a Creation not matched by any in the past or to come. He would live as a man, born to save us from certain destruction at our own doing. There were some prophecies about Him being slain, but I wasn't sure what much of that meant. Right now, I couldn't comprehend someone wanting to harm my baby.

*****

The smell of early morning was wonderful as I stepped out onto the porch. Ned and Ezra were giving me a ride to the bus station this morning, and I was nervous, but ready.

Elizabeth had stayed awake encouraging me most the

night, and was now asleep next to the baby. I had peeked in on them before I left, and received a warm hug from Zachariah, along with some letters he wanted me to take to my parents. I thanked him again for letting me come stay, and he kissed me on the forehead before I left.

Ezra picked up my suitcase and put it on the back of the truck, and then extended his hand to help me up onto the back.

"Dad says he'll take the bumps easier this time," he said looking at me.

"Thanks," I replied taking my hand from his as I sat down.

"You alright?" He asked with a smile.

"Are you?" I asked, truly feeling bad that I could be of no help to make him feel better. Ezra had really become a good friend these past three months.

He nodded. "Yeah, I'm good." Shutting the tailgate, he winked at me, stuck his hands in his pocket and went to get in the passenger seat.

Ned came out the house from speaking to Zachariah.

"It's going to be a great day, Mary," he said and made his way to the driver's side.

The trip to town took a little longer. True to his word, Ned took the turns easier and drove much slower. I kept my hand over the baby most of the ride, even though I was sure he was fine. Elizabeth had assured me several times the night before of how protected a little one would be in the womb. I was glad for her words as we jostled a bit, but I steadied myself against the side of the truck.

About forty minutes later we were at the bus station. There weren't too many people around, and Ezra took my suitcase as his dad helped me down from the truck. I felt slightly nauseous, but I was determined to appear as non-pregnant as possible.

Ezra walked off shortly after I checked in at the window, but his dad, Ned, stayed with me until they loaded us on the bus. I waved goodbye to him and my life here as we pulled out of the terminal. No matter what was about to happen, I was so thankful for the people here. My family and new friends had been such an encouragement to me, and I was riding into my destiny unafraid.

I sat down next to a kind looking woman. She introduced herself and said her name was Deborah. We talked for awhile, but after an hour, sleep overwhelmed me. The next thing I knew she waking me, asking if I wanted to get off the bus for a moment. We had made our first stop already, and everyone was going into the convenience store.

Aside from the fact that I had to pee, and I hated using the facilities on the bus, I knew I needed to get something to eat. Elizabeth had given me a few things, but I really wanted something different.

We were off the bus for about fifteen minutes, and when we returned to our seats, I scarfed down some food and listened to Deborah. She began to tell me some really cool stories about her life. Some of the things she said reminded me of stuff that Rebecca's brother, Adam, had done.

She was obviously a believer, and when she realized that I was, she began to talk about the prophecies. Much to my delight, she had a lot of information that I had never heard before, and my spirit danced within me at the news.

Apparently, there were some in the world that felt the prophecy of the Savior was soon to be realized. I lay my hand on my stomach as she spoke.

"And did you know," she said in a whisper. "I was at a university the other day, where a secret meeting was held. It was comprised of professors and students who believed in the word of the prophets. Many of us believe that the child will be born this year."

The gasp that escaped me was unintentional, and she looked at me with a really weird look. I realized my response seemed a bit dramatic, so I tried to explain.

"I've just never met anyone who talked so clearly about the prophecies," I explained. "To know that others believe it will be this year...is mind blowing."

She nodded. "Not only that," she said even quieter and looked around. "Some think that the child will be born in our region."

As confirmation of her words, my belly gurgled. My hand was already on my womb, so I pressed it firmly and he moved again. I smiled, and a warm peace overtook my body.

"Mary," Deborah touched my hand. "Call me crazy, but you literally look like you just saw the face of the Creator or something."

I blushed. "I'm just...I'm just so happy," I admitted.

She patted my hand. "As we all are, as we all will be, when He makes His appearance." Her voice faltered on the end of her sentence and tears formed in her eyes. She turned, wiping them away, and gazed out the window.

We sat for hours in silence, both moved by our conversation. It wasn't until the next stop that I realized an entire day had almost passed. In less than forty hours I'd be home. I had no idea what would happen the minute I stepped off the bus, but after talking with Deborah, I felt more confident.

After a few more stops, I finally fell into a deep sleep. I was so peaceful, and though I couldn't recall exactly what I had dreamed, I knew it had to have been of heaven. All I remembered was being in a place full of so much love and light. It was so real that when I awoke, disappointment loomed. Even though I had an important purpose for being here on earth, the place my mind had just been seemed to beckon me.

Deborah proved to be just the right person to journey with home. She still had more days to go on her trip, but I was so thankful for her energy. The faith she carried rippled off onto me. The more she spoke about the things to come, I felt as if I was getting a drink at the end of a hot day.

The bus driver announced that we were about to reach my destination. I gathered any lose items and put them in my back-pack and zipped it up. It took me a moment to realize the huge sigh I heard was from me. Deborah laughed.

"Mary," she said. "You look like you're about to face a firing squad." She nudged me in the arm. When I didn't laugh, she looked concerned. "Look, whatever it is, know that the Creator is with you. Your life has such purpose; I know it. The moment you walked onto the bus, I felt it. I don't know what you're facing, but I know you don't face it alone."

I reached over and took her hand. "Thanks, Deborah. That means so much to me."

The bus pulled into the drive and people began to stand up and grab their things. I steadied myself against the seat, as a wave of nausea rocked me. I gagged, but managed to force my stomach to behave.

Deborah stood up. "Here," she said handing me some-thing. I looked down to see a peppermint candy. Taking it from her I looked at her questioningly. She laughed. "I've been on the road of life a long while, Mary. Peppermint candy helps with nausea."

I was mortified, but she patted me on the back, smiled and

sat down in her seat. Somehow I placed one foot in front of the other and headed toward the entrance of the bus. My hands began to tremble, and I placed one hand over my stomach. Quickly I removed it, remembering how that was apparently one of the signs of a pregnant person.

Taking a deep breath, I sighed as I reached the light of the doorway. I could see people lined up outside the door, and I expected to see a familiar face at any moment. I wasn't sure who it was going to be. It was eleven at night, so my dad and mom might be here together.

My hand touched the coolness of the bus doorpost as I took the last step down to the ground. Readjusting my backpack on my shoulder, I scanned the line of people for a familiar face. Relief spread all over me as I looked into the eyes of my mother.

CHAPTER ELEVEN

NEVER SAY NEVER

"**MARY!**" She shouted.

Being in my mother's arms was such a comfort. All the changes and craziness of the last three months seemed to melt away in my mother's embrace.

"Sweetie," she exclaimed with joy. "It is so good to finally see you."

My father stepped up with my suitcase. "Hey, Mary girl. So glad you're home."

I hugged him and my tears fell on his shirt. He rubbed my hair like he always had since I was a little girl, and I felt so safe.

"I love you, daddy," I said against his chest.

I could feel the pause in his breath. He pulled me back a little bit and looked in my face. "I love you too, Mary." My dad stared into my eyes for a moment. "You haven't called me daddy in so many years, I think I had a flashback to the first time you came home from pre-school."

My mother laughed. "She must have really missed us, David." She hugged me again. "Now let's get home so she can rest. You must be so tired after the trip."

"Yeah," I admitted, wishing with all my heart that I could

just blurt out the truth. The most amazing thing had happened, and my family still had no idea.

I sat in the backseat of the car with my things. My mom turned around in her seat to talk to me.

"So, how is Beth? Everyone is still so baffled and elated that she had a son. Who would have thought at her age, that the Creator would see fit to give her such a precious gift?"

At the mention of Elizabeth's son, I felt like my chest got heavy. I sucked on the peppermint candy that Deborah had given me to distract my thoughts.

My dad chimed in. "That Zachariah has to be practically beside himself with pride. Not many old guys could pull it off."

"David," my mother said and hit him in the arm.

"Abigail, I'm only saying what everyone is thinking. He's the poster guy for virility. It's an honor to be related to him."

"Be that as it may," my mother responded. "Elizabeth is over fifty years of age, and that had to take some endurance. The Creator blessed them with this amazing birth for a reason, I just know it." With that she smiled at me and turned back around.

They talked back and forth about it all the way home. I didn't say a word...I couldn't. At any moment I knew the tears were coming. My realities were colliding. While I had been with my cousins, this part was so distant. Seeing my parents now, hearing them talk about the Creator and how blessed Elizabeth and Zachariah were, I was awestruck.

I was thankful the bus had arrived so late at night. After saying goodnight to my parents, I headed up to my room. The familiar decor hugged my soul, and I discarded my clothes and got beneath the covers. The tears came as furious as they had the last time I was here, but this time everything was different.

Right before coming up the stairs, my mother had said how happy she was that I was home. She mentioned that Joseph had spent the majority of the three months working on our new home, and how excited he was about my return. I had only talked to him twice, since I'd been gone, but he had written me every month.

He expressed himself in such an honest way in his letters. I had never in my life met someone so gentle and kind, and I could only hope that he would be as understanding of my current issue.

What would I say to everyone? Right now my stomach was hardly distinguishable, but at best, I had four more weeks before people started asking questions. At fifteen weeks, I was what Elizabeth called 'tiny' for my gestation. Esther had mentioned that perhaps I should see a doctor, but what would I tell them? I had no idea if this was a normal pregnancy, and I couldn't endanger my son by having him discovered.

Herod was a staunch persecutor of believers. Deborah had told me, with so many people talking about the Son of the Creator coming soon, Herod had actually begun raids. He wanted to know what information the believers had, and he had people studying all the prophecies.

A wave of fear went through me and I rocked back and forth. I had to believe that the plan for this child was foretold long before I was born. The Creator had to have known the state of the world, and I was merely a vessel for His use.

There was no mistaking that I was home. Today was a workday, and I heard my sister and brother in the hallway, arguing over who was going to take a shower first. I smiled and pulled the covers more securely around me. I didn't think my mother was expecting me to show up for breakfast, so I didn't pay much attention, when she yelled that breakfast was done.

Much to my surprise, about thirty minutes later, my sister, Amber, burst through my door.

"Mary," she whispered, but it was loud.

"Yeah," I responded.

She flipped on the light switch. "I told mom you were awake." Amber walked in and stood next to my bed.

"Are they eating downstairs?" I could smell pancakes.

"I think mom's just now getting done cooking. Colin is in a hurry, because he's meeting some friends before we have to go to the mill. Are you coming today? Mom said it was really late by the time they picked you up."

I yawned. "I might just plan on going tomorrow, but I'll come eat with you all."

Amber snickered. "Good, cause there's somebody downstairs that would burst if you don't." She giggled and trotted off down the hallway.

Sitting up I looked down at my stomach. With the covers on top I couldn't really see anything, so I pulled them down. He was still there, barely a bump, but noticeable for sure if I had no clothes on.

I decided to hop in the shower. The water felt amazing on my skin. Elizabeth and Zachariah didn't have the best water heater, so many of my showers were in lukewarm and only lasted a minute. I sighed with pleasure as the steam rose all around me, and for the first time in awhile, I felt completely relaxed.

Hunger hit me after I got done washing my hair, so I hurried and got out. Not wanting to waste time drying my hair, I got dressed and then just tied it up in a towel. The shower had definitely made me feel better, and I wasn't as nervous as I thought I'd be. I made my way downstairs.

The familiar sounds and smells greeted me, and I really was happy to be home. For some reason though, the kitchen seemed so far away as I began to walk toward it. I slowed my steps and took a deep breath before entering. I could already hear my mother.

"Yes, we are all so happy to have her home. She said the baby and Elizabeth are fine." She was on the phone. I should have known she'd be telling everyone about my safe arrival home. There wasn't much kept a secret in our culture.

"Hey, Mary," a man's voice startled me. I turned to see Joseph.

"Hi," I said and looked away from him.

"It's good to see you," he said, and I felt my face get warm.

My sister couldn't resist. "And she's happy that you get to see her," she responded.

"That's enough," my father chided her.

"I'm just helping her out, dad." She giggled and headed out the room.

Colin was wolfing down a mound of pancakes, but he paused long enough to say hello.

"Hey," was all he said and continued to eat.

"Hey, Colin," I replied and went to sit down at the table.

Joseph stood up for a moment and then sat back down when I did. I wouldn't have felt as awkward around him, except for the whole 'pregnant with the Creator's Son' thing. His letters the past few months were lengthy, and I felt like I knew him so much better than before.

My mother came over and set two plates down. One was full of food for Joseph, the other for me.

"Thanks, mom," I said, realizing that I was ravished with hunger.

"You're welcome, Mary." She turned and went back to the stove.

Joseph cleared his throat. "I'm glad you're back."

I nodded and smiled at him. "Me too," I responded and put another bite in my mouth.

"I know you just got back, but I was wondering if you'd like to come see the house."

Energy tickled up and down my body when he mentioned the house. It wasn't just another house he was building; it was our house.

"If it's okay with my dad," I answered looking over at my father. "Do you need me at the mill today?"

He shook his head. "No, it's fine. I thought you might want today to catch up on things. I'm sure your friends will want to talk and catch up as well."

"It's a date then," Joseph said with a smile. "How about I come pick you up in about two hours. I've got a quick job to check on, then I'll head back and get you."

"Okay," I said and smiled.

Joseph reached over and took my hand. "It's so good to see you."

I blushed. "You too, Joseph."

He let go of my hand and stood. "Thanks for the breakfast, Mrs. Meir.'"

"Anytime," my mom responded and waved to him with the dishrag.

"I'll talk to you later, David," he said to my father.

My dad just nodded and went back to reading the paper.

"Mary," he said with a nod.

"I'll be ready," I said as he left out the door.

He turned back toward me and waved with a smile.

After breakfast my family left for the mill. I watched them drive off, and wondered what they would all be doing right now if they knew. None of them had any idea that I was pregnant, and it baffled me that it could be true without anyone seeing it.

Taking the towel off my head, I went upstairs to blow dry my hair. It had gotten longer over the past few months, and my arms began to ache holding the blow dryer so long. I unpacked some things from my suitcase and emptied my backpack. The last three months and two weeks had gone by so fast, but I was so thankful for them.

The clock on the wall said, eight o'clock, so I expected Joseph a little before ten. Since we were engaged, there wasn't any issue with us being left alone. As Esther had pointed out before, in my culture, the engagement day with the elders was considered married. As far as anyone in my community was concerned, the wedding was just a formal celebration of what had already taken place.

I decided to lie down for an hour. I grabbed a pillow and headed out to the backyard. The bench beneath the trees was a perfect spot. As long as I rested when I could, I didn't think anyone would pick up on my tiredness being attributed to my hormones having gone nuts.

"Mary?" I recognized Joseph's voice immediately.

I opened my eyes to see his handsome face above me.

"Sorry," I apologized. "I fell asleep."

He smiled. "No apologies necessary. "You looked like an angel asleep. I could have watched you all day."

My face got hot and I knew I'd blushed by the expression on his face. I realized I had been lying on my back, with my hands on my stomach, so I tried to sit up quickly. Joseph noticed what I was attempting to do and extended his hand to help me.

Swinging my legs off of the bench, I let go of his hand to reach up and smooth down my hair.

"You look fine," he said with a smile.

"You say that," I teased. "But in this family, people have been known to let you walk around half a day with toilet paper stuck to your foot."

Joseph laughed loudly. It echoed in the wind. For some reason it made me feel really safe.

"Your family is rather humorous. I have to admit, your dad got me good the other day."

"Really?" I asked standing up. "Anything you care to share?"

He stood up as we began to walk toward the house. "He told me you had called and said you weren't coming back. That you'd met someone else."

I stopped walking. "That doesn't sound too funny, but I can totally see my dad torturing you like that."

Joseph shook his head. "I thought at first that he was joking, but then he kept it up all day. He had no idea that I'd almost driven out to get you."

Looking into his eyes, I wanted to tell him. I wanted to tell him everything that had happened. This wasn't fair to him. Here he was, standing just inches away from me, openly adoring. How was I going to tell him I was pregnant?

"Mary, are you alright?" He asked very concerned.

I felt sick. A wave of nausea hit me, and there was no calming it down. Right there in front of Joseph, I hurled.

There wasn't time for me to be embarrassed. The puking was so intense it frightened me a little. Joseph stood beside me holding my hair away from my face, as I wretched over and over again. All the contents of breakfast were spilling out on the lawn, and I couldn't stop it.

Finally, a few gagging refluxes later, the world stopped being on fire and I felt my stomach relax. I could only imagine what Joseph was thinking, but I didn't have long to wait.

"Do I need to call you mom?" He asked desperately.

"No!" I responded louder than I'd intended. "I'm alright." I tried to slow my breathing.

"But you're sick, Mary. Do I need to take you to the doctor or something?"

I finally looked up at him. His face was washed with concern.

"I'm okay, Joseph, really I am."

He helped me up the stairs to the back of the house and then opened the door.

"Let me go wash my face," I offered, and walked down the hallway to the bathroom.

This was nuts. How was I going to explain what had just happened? Joseph was sure to say something to my family about it. His face showed how much of a crisis he thought it was. I had to do something quickly to calm the situation.

I splashed water on my face and dried it off with a towel. After rinsing my mouth several times, I brushed my hair and put it in a tie. My cheeks looked a little pale, but I rubbed them with the towel and they appeared pinker.

Joseph was standing right outside the bathroom door when I opened it.

"You okay?" He asked reaching out to rub my arm.

"Yeah, I'm totally okay. I haven't had mom's pancakes in awhile. Maybe I just got used to the stuff out at the farm." It was the only thing that wasn't a lie that I could think of.

He seemed to accept that. "Well do you want to postpone going to the house? We can always do it another day."

Shaking my head I took his hand. "No, I really want to see it. Mom tells me it's almost finished."

That brought a huge smile to his face. "Yeah. I worked really hard while you were gone. I know all this is such a crazy change, and I thought you'd feel more comfortable, if you had some input about the house."

"That's sweet, Joseph," I replied, and for the first time initiated a hug.

It wasn't like hugging my father. Joseph smelled really good, like fresh wood after a rain. He was obviously surprised at my gesture, but when I kept holding onto him, he put his arms around me and embraced me back. I took a deep breath, and for some reason relaxed.

We stood there for a moment, neither one of us saying a word. He began to sway back and forth from side to side, and it was like dancing. There wasn't anything weird about it, and it encouraged me that everything would be okay.

The hall clock chimed and we both took a step back. He still had his arms around me, and I looked up into his face and smiled. Joseph took his arms from around me and grabbed my hand.

"Are you ready to go then?" He asked.

I nodded, too overwhelmed to trust myself to answer verbally.

The ride to the house was about twenty minutes. I was so glad that my family would be within driving distance of my new home. He had to have spent nearly every hour since I was gone out here. The structure was completely done on the outside, all the windows were in and he'd even finished the driveway.

"Wow," I said and looked over at him. "Joseph, it's beautiful."

He looked pleased by my response and gently squeezed my hand.

"It's only two bedrooms for now, but you've got a really big kitchen with huge windows. I know how you love the outdoors."

I smiled. "You do?" I asked as he pulled up and turned off the truck.

"Yeah," he answered and turned to me. "I remember a few years ago, when you were around thirteen. It was winter, and your mom couldn't get you to come in the house and put a coat on. It was Thanksgiving, and for the first time ever it snowed."

"I remember that," I said. "And I ran outside with no shoes on, nor a coat." I laughed. "My dad finally convinced her that I wouldn't die from a cold, so she left me alone. It was awesome."

Joseph got out and went around the front of the truck. After opening my door, he took my hand again and we walked up to the front door.

"I painted it this color green so that it's sort of hidden within the environment."

"I like it," I said smoothing my hand down the pillar on the porch. He opened the front door, and I took a step forward, but Joseph stopped me.

"Hold on a minute," he said seriously.

"What?" I asked, looking down to make sure nothing was obviously showing.

"We've got to do this the right way."

Before I could register what he was doing, Joseph easily scooped me up off my feet.

"Joseph!" I said surprised. "Put me down!" I giggled despite my request.

"Never," he said so sweetly; my heart felt the words.

He walked through the door, and I leaned my head on his chest and inhaled. I would never grow tired of this smell. Joseph set me down as easily as he had picked me up, and walked across the room.

"I thought you might want to decide the wall color," he offered.

I looked around the new living room in wonder. "This is really nice. How did you get this all done in three months?"

He beamed with pride. "Let's just say I was...motivated. Not much else for a guy to do with his wife gone half way across the country."

When he said 'wife,' I felt all sorts of emotion burst from inside of me. He could tell by my face that his words had impacted me, even though I wasn't quite sure which way.

"Mary...I didn't mean to put pressure on you. I just...well, according to the law we're already husband and wife."

The room seemed like it got incredibly hot. "It's okay. You just never, I mean...I guess I'm getting used to the idea is all."

Joseph walked back over to me and took my hands. "I know this is all going really fast, but I don't have any expectations. I'm really proud that you want to be my wife, Mary. I just wanted to express how serious I take the responsibility. Till death do us part...you know?"

I swallowed and felt myself squeeze his hands. Did he really mean that? If he knew about the baby, would he still really mean that?

Chapter Twelve

Impact

FOR the next two weeks I truly enjoyed being home. Joseph was a frequent visitor at the dinner table, and each day I saw him he grew dearer to me. I prayed every day for guidance. There were so many times that I wanted to tell my mother. Once, she made a remark about how much food I had eaten, and my sister joked about how I'd be too fat to fit my wedding dress.

I rolled over one night in my sleep and it was actually uncomfortable. The next day I realized that my little belly had gotten bigger. I stood sideways in the mirror, and without a shirt on, you could definitely see that I was pregnant. At seventeen weeks, I was still a little small, but it no longer looked like I'd just eaten too much food.

The baby moved more now. Once while I was watching television, he kicked me so hard I laughed aloud. Everyone looked at me weird, but assumed I'd gotten a case of the giggles from watching the show.

Rebecca was getting back today from visiting her aunt and uncle. She'd already called and asked to come over, and I hesitantly agreed. Out of everyone I knew here, accidentally telling her about the baby was highly possible.

After doing paperwork for my father at the mill, I got a ride back to the house. Rebecca was coming over around three, so I ate a late lunch and waited for her to arrive.

On the table were all the school supplies that my mother had brought the last few days. School was going to start next week, and I was going along with things and planned to attend.

This year I wasn't in any sports, so I figured I'd be able to conceal the baby for quite awhile. No one would think anything about me wearing a jacket in school, because the air conditioner was always on full blast.

I heard Rebecca rap on the front door and yelled for her to come in. She found me sitting in the living room with the television on.

"Hey, Becs," I said standing up to greet her.

"Hey, Mary," she replied and walked into my open arms. We hugged for a moment, and then sat down.

She was absolutely beaming with news, I could tell. "So..." I began. "Spill it. You look like you're about to burst."

Rebecca laughed and put up her left hand. "I'm engaged!" She exclaimed.

"What?" I asked excitedly. "When? Who?"

Her smile was amazing. "His name is Luke, and I met him this summer. He was visiting from across the country, and decided to make his home here. One day we got to talking, and my dad took notice and began to ask about him. He's from a really good family, Mary. I'm so happy."

"When are you getting married?" I asked, completely shocked, but happy for her.

"Our year wait began just last month. I'll be married next year at the end of June."

I shook my head. "Wow, I can't believe this, Becs. Both of us, married women." We both laughed.

"I know," she said and leaned back on the couch. "I'm just so happy, Mary. I didn't want you to hear about it from a soul, so we waited to tell anyone here in town. We had the elder meeting at my aunt and uncle's house."

"That's why you were gone?"

She nodded. "Yeah, you know how everyone tells everything here. Well, my mom also wanted to wait until my cousin Julia's wedding was done. She's been waiting for this so long, she's already got half the plans done. Speaking of which, have you picked a venue and all that?"

"For what?" I asked, completely baffled.

"For your wedding day, silly." She hit me on the leg. "What's wrong with you? You're getting hitched sooner than me."

"Oh," I said, making sure the throw blanket on my lap was in place. "I just hadn't really thought about it yet. Joseph did take me to see the house though." I smiled, proud of his efforts.

"I heard about your house," she said kind of strange. Rebecca smiled, but it was as if all the energy had changed in the room.

"What's that supposed to mean?" I asked.

She shrugged. "Nothing, just that I've heard about your house." Her body language dictated something very off.

"Becs, what's the deal?" I used the remote to turn the television off.

Rebecca looked annoyed. "My mother can't stop talking about your house. Ever since he started working on that stupid thing, my mom has talked about how blessed you are to be starting off with a brand new home. Well," she scoffed. "I'd have a brand new home waiting for me, if I'd snagged a carpenter."

"Rebecca, what's your deal?" I asked getting upset.

Sighing, she stood up. "Nothing, Mary, just forget it. Anyway, I wanted to let you know I'm not going to be able to walk to school with you this year. Luke wants me to focus on our family, and I think it's a good idea."

I stood up. "So you're not going to school?"

"Isn't that what I just said?" She asked smartly. "Look, not everyone is like you. You've got things figured out and always end up handling situations with ease. I can't focus on something like school and a husband at the same time. So for now, I've got to take a break. Mom says sometimes in our tradition, people will even cut the year period and live together earlier. I really like Luke, and I'm ready to begin my life with him."

Raising my hands, I walked toward her. "Don't get me wrong, Becs. I'm not condemning you or anything. I'm just surprised that's all. I pray you nothing but the best union, and I sincerely mean it." My voice ended in a slight cry.

She looked like she felt bad, but was being stubborn. "Thanks, Mary, and by the way, could you just call me Rebecca? Luke thinks Becs is a childish name."

A slap across my face would have hurt less. She was acting as if she couldn't stand me. I could only imagine what she would be like, when she found out about the baby.

"Sure thing," I replied to her request. "I love you, Rebecca."

My words washed over her face and she broke. "I'm sorry, Mary," she stuttered out. "It's just...I'm just overwhelmed by everything. I don't know how you do it." She began to cry.

I walked up to my friend and embraced her.

"Its just faith. We have to believe that the Creator is with us, and that everything will turn out okay. You like Luke, don't you?" She nodded. "Then get to know him and focus on that.

You're probably right about school. It would be difficult to do both, especially if you two are going to move in together soon."

She nodded and grabbed her purse. "I'm sorry I made such a mess out of this," she apologized. "I really just came over to see how you were doing and tell you my news." A kind look spread across her face. "How are you doing...with everything?"

"I'm fine," I replied thinking about my son. "We're doing good."

"That's awesome." She looked around. "Well, I've got to go. I'll call you later. I'm going to meet Luke at the hardware store. He's getting a place over on Sutton fixed up for us. It'll probably take awhile, and it's not the greatest, but we'll fix it up."

"Can I come by and see it some time?" I offered.

"Of course," she said and waved.

Turning she walked down the hall. I could hear the front door shut behind her, and I sank down onto the couch. Had the entire world gone nuts? Rebecca had been my best friend for years, and I had no idea what had gotten her so riled up. I lay my hand across my belly. Thank the Creator I didn't tell her. I could only imagine what she would have done.

When my family returned home, I told them the news about Rebecca. My mom was happy for her, but immediately concerned about me walking to school by myself. I was actually concerned, because I thought about the baby, and wondered how long I would be able to walk the distance.

Joseph came over later and had dinner with us. If he wasn't at the house for breakfast, he always showed up at dinnertime. No longer needing an invite, he usually just knocked on the door and came in.

Tonight, after everyone had gone to bed, he and I sat on

the couch and watched television. We talked off an on about his day and mine, and I explained to him about how upset my talk with Rebecca had made me.

"She was really mad," I explained. "I mean, I understand how overwhelming all this can be, but she really seemed upset about the house."

Joseph sighed and took my hand. "Unfortunately, Mary, not everyone is happy just because you're happy. I know that Luke guy, and he seems pretty nice. But they're not starting off in our circumstances. Although I'm not the richest man, we'll have a comfortable beginning with my business."

I ran my finger along the calluses on his hand. "And you work very hard for that business, Joseph. The house is beautiful."

He reached over and swept my hair from my cheek. "Like I said, I had some motivation."

His hand lingered a moment on my face and I felt warm instantly. He sat staring into my eyes, and I felt lost within his. How had I not noticed him sooner? The tenderness that he exuded washed over me, and I felt so close to him. A question popped into my mind.

"Joseph?" I asked.

"Yes, Mary," he responded and put his hand down.

"Do you love me?" I couldn't believe the words came out my mouth.

Without hesitation, Joseph looked intently into my eyes. "More than I will ever be able to put into words. I love you, Mary."

I felt hot tears roll down my cheeks and he reached up and wiped them away.

"Why?" I asked as I began to cry.

He shook his head slightly. "It doesn't make sense really.

One day, when I came to visit your dad with your Uncle Matt, I looked over and saw you playing. You were around twelve then, so I was seventeen. All of a sudden, this feeling of protectiveness rose up inside of me. I felt the need to make sure you were okay." He paused for a moment and wiped more tears from my face. "Then over the years, the feeling changed. It was the day after your fifteenth birthday. We were all at the lake, and I heard you laugh. I realized at that moment, that I didn't want a day to go by without hearing you laugh."

Tears poured down my face now. I reached up with both my arms and grabbed him like a life preserver. I could only hope that the words he was saying were true. The Creator had to have made this man for me, to be the earthly father of His Son.

"Mary," he whispered on my hair.

"Yes," I said softly.

"I love you, but you're suffocating me."

"Oh," I said and relaxed my arms around the top of his shoulders.

He stroked my hair down my back. "Now, as much as I'm enjoying this moment, I better go." Joseph pushed me gently from him, but I didn't let go. "Mary?" He asked and squeezed me one last time.

"Yes," I said with a sigh.

He laughed. "I've got to go. We're doing a job just south of here at five in the morning."

"Oh, I'm sorry," I apologized and sat back from him.

Joseph took my hands. "But I was wondering if you wanted to go see the house again tomorrow. I've got the paint up in the living room."

"Yeah, of course." I smiled and allowed him to pull me to standing.

"I'll see you tomorrow then," he said and kissed the top of my head.

You would have thought he kissed me smack on the lips. My knees actually felt weak.

"Okay," I replied as he took a step back.

"You alright?" He asked with a smirk.

"Uh, huh," I replied and sat back down.

"I'll see you around three then," he said and turned down the hall.

The door clicked behind him and I leaned back on the couch. I was falling in love with this man. There was no doubt about it. My son kicked and reality washed over me. Yeah, I was falling in love with a man, while carrying the Son of the Creator. Was that even okay?

I sat up and folded the blanket I'd been sitting under. After putting it away in the hall closet, I climbed the stairs and went to bed. I was cautiously happy. I knew eventually things would take a drastic turn, but I wasn't sure when.

* * * * *

The day started off fairly routine. I went to the mill with my family, finished the paperwork by two and got a ride home. It was so hot outside, and the dust at the mill was flat out crazy. Before going with Joseph, I decided to take a shower and change.

I opted for a loose fitting white shirt that I'd worn all summer. It still had enough room in it, plus it was gathered at the bottom. Looking in the mirror, I was proud of my disguise, and even when I smoothed the shirt down, the gathering hid the baby bump.

Joseph showed up right at three, and I was eager to see the house. We listened to music on the way there, and I was pleasantly surprised that he could carry a tune.

Laughing, we pulled up to the house in good spirits, and I got out the car before he had time to open the door. I bent down and picked up some gravel from the drive, and when he came around my side, I tossed a stone at him.

"This is new," I said and kicked the gravel.

He dodged the rock. "Yeah, it's just in this small part of the yard. We laid the drive awhile ago, but with heavy trucks going back and forth, I laid some gravel down."

"Heavy trucks?" I asked. "Why? I thought the house was almost done." I turned around to look at the house.

He walked up beside me and took my hand. "It wasn't for the house," he replied sheepishly and began to lead me around the side of the house.

Halfway around he stopped. "Okay, close your eyes, and no peeking."

"Okay," I agreed.

We walked a little further before he stopped. "Alright, now open them."

Slowly I opened my eyes. There before me, was the most beautiful gazebo.

"Oh, Joseph," I whispered. "What have you done?"

It wasn't just a gazebo. It had a floor made of concrete that was painted or stained a beautiful russet color. Right in the middle was a fountain!

He laughed. "I got kind of bored," he said and spun me around. "It's my wedding present to you," he admitted.

I let go of his hand and walked forward. "Thank you," I said. "Thank you, so much." Walking to the edge of the beautiful fountain, I let my hand rest at the base of the trickling water. "This is beautiful." My voice caught in my throat.

Joseph came to my side. "Like I said before, I know how you like to be outside." He reached up and pulled on a rope. A tarp dropped down from the top and covered one side of it. "This way, even if it rains, you can stay out here."

"Wow," was all I could say. I looked around at the benches, the little statues of animals and the plants. This had to have taken awhile to do. "When did you have time to do this?" I asked looking over at him.

He shrugged. "The last two weeks I couldn't sleep so good." Joseph smirked and walked closer to me.

"What's that?" I asked pointing to a hose on the ground.

Looking down he moved it over. "That's just the hose we used to get your fountain started last night."

"You came here last night?"

"Only for a minute. I don't live that far from here." He stopped and looked at me with a question. "You haven't ever seen where I live now, have you?"

I shook my head.

"Well," he said excitedly. "That's something we'll remedy right now."

He took my hand and we walked back to the truck.

"But I haven't seen the paint on the walls," I said and laughed.

"We'll, come back by," he answered and opened the truck door for me.

I was excited as we drove. I'd never thought to ask where

Joseph lived. He was always at my house, so it never crossed my mind.

We pulled onto a residential street not too far away, but opposite of the direction we would have taken to my house. About ten minutes later he pulled up to a tiny house on a lot.

"This is it," he said.

It looked like a little log cabin. It didn't really fit with any house in the neighborhood, but I could tell that was the point. We got out and walked up to the door.

"Now, mind you," he began. "I've been in this bachelor pad since I was sixteen. So it's not like it's all cozy for a girl."

"I can handle it," I said and put my hand on the knob.

He laughed and took out his keys. "It's not unlocked, Mary. This isn't the safest neighborhood in the world."

I looked around behind me. "It looks alright," I said supportively.

Joseph pushed the door open, and gestured for me to go before him. I smiled and went in the door.

The first thing I saw was a huge table in the middle of the room.

"Dinning room?" I questioned.

He smiled. "Not exactly. I lay house plans on it." He took my hand and led me the short distance to the table. "See, here are the plans for your gazebo."

I looked down at the lines and graphs on the table. "Uh, okay. Let's just say I wasn't the best student in math."

Joseph laughed. "It's just the graphs that are the most complicated. If I'm off on the scale by a centimeter, someone's house might fall."

The room also had a little couch in it. I saw another door just down a hall, and the tiny kitchen was just to my right.

"What's through there?" I asked and pointed toward the door.

"The bathroom," he said. "And obviously the kitchen is right there. That's it though. Just this room, the kitchen and the bathroom."

"Where do you sleep?" I asked looking around.

"Right there." He pointed to the couch. "Honestly, I'm not here long enough to warrant a bed. But don't worry, we'll have a big one."

His entire being looked mortified at his last comment. I already knew I had turned almost purple with embarrassment, and he looked lost as to how to handle the comment. I was never more thankful than to hear thunder than this moment.

"Is it supposed to rain today?" I asked going over to the window.

"Yeah," he answered softly. I knew he was still embarrassed, so I tried to act casual.

"It'll be good for the grass. We haven't had rain for a couple of days."

Joseph came and stood beside me, as a round of thunder rippled across the sky and it began to rain.

"Yeah," he said again, but took my hand. "Sorry about that, Mary. I didn't mean...well, not that I don't want to be with you, but I didn't...." His sentence trailed off and I felt my entire face flame.

"I know what you meant," I said. "It's okay."

We watched the rainfall for a moment.

He cleared his throat. "Hey, you want to see something cool?"

"Yeah," I said, relieved the subject had changed.

"Come with me."

Joseph took my hand and led me to the kitchen. There was a door that led to the outside. The rain wasn't too bad, and he looked back at me as we exited toward a grove of trees.

We ran hand in hand, until we reached the shelter of the thick leaves. Joseph let go of my hand and trotted over to a huge oak tree. He pointed and I looked up to see the most amazing little tree house.

"That is cool," I said and giggled. "Did you build that too?"

"Yeah," he replied and began to climb up the rope ladder. He reached the top in no time and extended his hand down to help me climb.

Excited, I reached up, as he effortlessly pulled me almost all the way up. There wasn't a door on the tree house, but it still managed to be cozy despite the bits of rain that made their way in.

We sat talking for a while, and I learned more about Joseph and his family. He wasn't originally from here, and most of his kinfolk were thousands of miles away. He'd been gifted in woodwork and carpentry since a young age, so it was only natural that he had become a carpenter.

He started working on buildings around the age of sixteen, and then at the age of eighteen he started his own business and became a contractor. I was amazed at how smart and diligent he had been to prosper without much help from his own family.

After an hour, I realized as wonderful as this moment was, I had to pee. It was still hot though it was raining, and I really had sweat a lot while in the tree house. I hinted around about needing to use the restroom, so Joseph climbed down and reached up to help me down the ladder.

As I reached for him, I lost my balance, and instead of

coming down slowly, I was thrown forcefully downward. The last thing I remembered was hearing him yell my name.

CHAPTER THIRTEEN

COMPLICATIONS

I woke up at the sound of my mother's frantic voice. Shaking my head to enter the place I could hear, I realized immediately that I was no longer outside by the tree house. I was being wheeled down a hallway, and the lights flashed quickly overhead.

"Mary!" I heard my mother's voice over all the other noise. I tried to respond back, but I was dizzy.

Reaching up, I felt something sticky on my forehead. I pulled my fingers down and realized blood was coming from my head. My hand went immediately to my stomach. I could still feel the roundness of the baby, and then I thought about the people pushing my bed. I tried to sit up, but a hand restrained me.

"Let me go," I finally managed to say, but it sounded like it was echoing instead of normal voice.

"Lie down, Mary," my mother said.

I fought against the dizziness and it began to settle. I tried to sit up again despite what she said.

"Mary," she said softer this time. "They need to make sure you're okay. Lie down, sweetheart."

"No," I said, pushing hands away from me. The dizziness left me, and I looked over to see two women and my mother.

One of the women patted my hand. "You fell and we need to make sure you're okay."

I shook my head at her. "No, I'm fine. What's up with my head though?" I asked looking around.

She looked closer at my head. "Looks like you might need a couple of stitches. Could have been a lot worse I heard. You fell from a considerable height."

"Where's Joseph?" I asked looking toward my mother.

"He and your father are out in the waiting room. He brought you here and we met him as quick as we could."

I swallowed and moved my arms and legs around. I felt my son move around; immediately I felt relieved.

"Did he say how I fell?" I asked, moving around to make sure I didn't break anything.

My mom smiled. "That's the only funny part about it," she said. "He said you came flying out of that tree so quickly, and the only thing he could do was try to catch you. We think your head got cut by a stick, but he took the impact of your fall on his own body. He said it was equivalent to when he played football in high school."

I laughed, relieved that I hadn't landed on my stomach.

The nurse came and took my blood pressure. "Everything looks to be in order. Are you feeling anything, pain, nausea, the baby move?"

Her words were frozen like ice cycles that hung in mid-air.

My mother laughed. "Baby?" She smirked. "Mary's not having a baby." She looked over at me, but obviously didn't get the response she thought she would.

The nurse looked at the other nurse, who looked down at

my chart. The other lady nodded her head, and then they both looked over at me.

My mother stood up and took a step closer to me.

"Mary?"

So many thoughts swirled around in my mind. I thought I'd have a little more time before I needed to tell everyone. Laying my hand on my stomach, tears began to stream down my face. Even though I'd done nothing wrong, and I carried a secret that many had foretold, I felt horrible.

"Mom...I..."

"Mary, what are you saying?" My mother's voice trembled.

The two women looked at one another and quietly exited the room.

My mother walked over and took my hand.

"Look at me, Mary. You tell me...you tell me right now. Are you...pregnant?"

Biting my lip, I thought words wouldn't be enough in a moment like this. I let go of her hand and stood up. I reached down and pulled up the bottom of my shirt and slipped it off. There was no mistaking my pregnant belly.

She sat down on the chair in front of me and reached out her hand. I was in the eighteenth week, and I looked like it. There was no way to deny what she saw and felt, but I knew I had to explain.

"Joseph," she said. "Does Joseph know what he has done? All you had to do was wait one year, and if he had wanted you sooner, he should have said so. We would have announced it properly, Mary."

I shook my head. "Joseph doesn't know, mom."

"But he's the one I hold responsible, Mary." She gasped.

"Was this the reason he had the idea for you to go to Elizabeth's early? Were you two together before the engagement?"

Grabbing the gown that lay on the table, I slipped it on and sat down on the bed. My mother looked like she was going to have a heart attack.

"Mom," I said raising my voice. "No, it's not the reason. He doesn't even know...I've never slept with him."

At that my mother looked like she was going to fall off the chair.

"What are you trying to tell me, Mary? What are you saying?" She stood up and ran to the door. "David!" She yelled. "David, come quick!"

I stood up and backed across the room. This was not how I wanted to tell them. This was not going according to any plan I had imagined.

My father ran breathlessly to the room.

"What is it, Abigail! Is she alright?" He stepped in the room and she shut the door.

She walked over to me and took my hand. "Something's happened to our Mary," she cried.

"I know, Abby, but the doctor said the fall wasn't too bad," he explained.

Shaking her head she reached for his hand. He took hers. "No, David, not that. Our Mary has been...she's been..."

"I'm pregnant, dad," I said and looked straight at him.

He stood for a minute looking confused, and then you could see realization wash over him.

"Does Joseph know about this? I mean, why did he not wait?" My father began to pace around the room.

"Daddy, he's not the father." I said the sentence very matter of fact.

"Not the father?" He asked almost hateful. "What do you mean, he's not the father? Did someone...who did this to you, Mary?" He grabbed my arms so hard I winced and he let go.

"No one," I said walking away.

"What do you mean?" He screamed at me. "Someone took advantage of you, Mary, and we must know who it is!"

I imagined at this moment I would be hysterical, but this calm peace fell on me. I turned and looked at both my parents.

"Joseph is not the father, nor is any man."

I closed my eyes and began to tell them a story. The story that had begun the day after my engagement, when the angel had shown up in the greenhouse.

For twenty minutes they sat speechless; my mother with tears streaming down her face. For a moment I had a little hope that they might believe me as I talked. It was an incredible story, one that no one would even consider to make up.

When I got done, my father stood and walked over to the window.

"Mary, I want to believe what you have said. I want to believe you for many reasons, but do you realize what you are saying?"

I stood and walked over to him. "I wouldn't lie about something like this." I took his hand and put it on my stomach. "He's here, daddy. I don't know why the Creator chose me, but He did. No matter if you believe me or not, it's the truth."

My dad embraced me, and I felt my mother come up behind me.

"We believe you, Mary," she said and stroked my hair. "But I'm afraid no one else will. When the elders learn of your pregnancy, there will be consequences spoken."

"I know, mom." I turned to face her. "But the Creator

knew the law before this happened. I have to believe that He will take care of us."

Wiping the tears from her eyes she sighed. "And Joseph. What will he say about all this?" She looked over to my father.

I had never seen my father cry. In the fifteen years of being on this earth, I'd never seen him cry. Now, tears poured unashamed from his eyes.

"He will have to be told right away." He took my hands. "Mary, the prophecies say that you are the one that will be called blessed of all women. If this is true, then no harm will come to you. However, you must tell Joseph. He has a right to know, and to make his choice."

"I believe he loves me, daddy.'"

My father sighed and stroked my hand. "I believe he does, Mary. But this is not a light thing. He must be allowed a choice."

The doctor finally came in and they did an ultrasound of the baby. He looked perfect. She said everything checked out fine, and that nothing was wrong with the baby. My parents stood by my side, completely baffled by what they had just learned. When my mother saw the ultrasound screen, she wept and my dad had to keep her from collapsing to the floor.

After another fifteen minutes, I was discharged. All that time, Joseph had been waiting in the lobby. My father had went out and told him that I was going to be okay, but he refused to leave until he got to see me.

As I walked out, anxiety gave birth to fear, and it spread all over me. I started to tremble, and my father steadied me as we neared Joseph.

Joseph looked ten years older. The worry on his face began to lift, when he saw my face, and he rushed over to us.

"Mary, you're alright," he said and took my hand.

I smiled, but it was shaky. "Thanks for catching me," I said, trying to ease the tension in myself.

"Anytime," he replied. "I was so relieved that you didn't break anything."

My mom made a suggestion that surprised me.

"Joseph, why don't you meet us at the house in an hour for dinner. That way Mary will have a chance to get cleaned up, and then you two can talk."

"Yes, of course," he replied and let go of my hand.

The three of them walked me to the car, and Joseph opened the back door so I could get in. He tapped the window as we drove off down the street, and another wave of tears erupted from my mother.

I could understand. I had almost four months of getting used to the idea, but they had only had an hour. Things could have gone much worse under the circumstances. I was just thankful that the baby hadn't been harmed in my fall, and my parents believing me made things even better.

When we got home, my mom helped me get out of my things and I took a shower. She dried my hair for me with the blow dryer, still crying every so often. I could see she would be okay, but this was really hard for her.

Over the years she had been satisfied that my family had good standing in the community. I knew now, even though she wasn't saying it, that she was concerned for many reasons.

I began to explain to her about how the angel told me about Elizabeth being pregnant, and that was the reason I left early. She felt a little better at that explanation, but I knew she was preoccupied with damage control.

And hour later, Joseph showed up. He came in smiling with a handful of flowers. I thanked him, handed them to my mother, and then asked him to come to my father's office with me. He looked concerned, but I smiled, trying to console him.

The last time we had been in the office together was a hard conversation, and this one was going to prove to be even more challenging. I could only hope that he believed the words he had spoken to me previously. I had to believe he loved me.

I sat on the tiny couch and motioned for him to sit beside me. When he sat down, I turned to face him, taking both his hands in mine.

"Joseph," I began hesitantly.

He sighed. "Whatever you have to say, it's okay, Mary. I was careless today, and you have every right to be upset. I shouldn't have climbed the tree house in the rain."

I looked away from him then. This was too much. He was apologizing to me for falling on top of him, an act that probably saved the life of my unborn child.

"Stop," I said, trying to maintain my composure. I couldn't fall apart right now. I had to tell him.

"But, Mary, I..." I put my hand on his mouth.

"What I'm about to tell you has nothing to do with the tree house and my fall. I need you to listen."

He nodded his head so I removed my hand.

"I know we are just getting to know one another really, but I have come to care for you, Joseph. I don't know if that means I love you, but I can't imagine going through my life with anyone other than you."

Joseph's face relaxed, and a burden seemed to have lifted off his shoulders.

Starting with the greenhouse incident, I poured out the story. Joseph looked completely dumbfounded the more I talked, and at one point he let go of my hands. As soon as I got to the part about going to Elizabeth's house, he stood up.

"So you're...pregnant?" He asked accusingly.

"Yes," I answered, immediately concerned.

He backed up. "You knew...you knew the whole summer?"

I nodded this time, realizing that this was not going well.

Joseph took another step back, looking at me as if I'd taken a dagger and stabbed him in the heart.

"Mary, are you seriously telling me that an angel came to you, told you the Creator would use you like this, and now you're pregnant?" He kind of smirked on the end, but when I nodded my head without smiling, he looked like lightening had struck him.

Just like my mom, I figured the best thing to do was show him. I had purposefully put on a smaller shirt before entering the room. I stood up and smoothed down the front of my shirt and turned sideways. There was no mistaking what he was seeing.

Joseph stumbled backward, hitting the door.

"What?" He asked in disbelief. "How could you do this, Mary? He stormed forward so suddenly it frightened me. Joseph grabbed me by both my arms and looked into my face. "Tell me the truth," he said in agony. "Who did this to you? Are you...are you in love with another man?"

Protectively I dropped my hands around the baby. Tears streamed from my eyes.

"No, Joseph, there is no one else." I sobbed. "I know what you must think of me, but it's all true."

He let go of me and disgust was the only adjective that seemed appropriate to describe his look. Joseph backed away from me and looked down at my stomach.

"You're going to stand there and lie to me? Don't I deserve better than that, Mary?" He asked angrily. "I love you, and this is what you do to me?"

Thunder echoed so loud I jumped. The sound of rain began to pour down on the house. Before I could answer he stormed out the room. I ran after him.

"Joseph!" I yelled, but he didn't turn around. He was moving fast, but I grabbed his arm. He jerked it away from me and kept walking. "Joseph!" I screamed now, and I felt my mother's arms go around me.

"Let him go, Mary," she said restraining me.

"No," I said somewhat pushing her to get out the door.

Joseph had made it to his truck, but I ran to catch him before he could open the door.

"Listen to me," I pleaded as rain began to soak my clothes. He hit the door of the truck with his fist.

"Stay away from me, Mary," he said coldly.

"Joseph," I reached out and grabbed the front of his shirt, but he jerked away from me again.

I saw my father walking my direction and clung onto Joseph with all my might. He wouldn't look at me and instead tried to take my hands off of him. I could see his clinched jaw.

"Joseph," I cried. "Please, please don't leave like this," I begged loudly.

My father had reached us and grabbed me around my waist.

"Mary, sweetheart, let him go," he said sternly.

The driveway was slippery as I fought against his pull, and my feet kept sliding around, but I refused to let go. I yelled even louder, but Joseph continued to look away from me and try to take my hands from the folds of his shirt.

Finally Joseph managed to undo my fingers, and my father

jerked me away. I cried even harder, but to no avail. Joseph got in his truck and gunned the engine, peeling away on the slippery streets, until he was out of sight.

I fell to the ground in a heap. My father held me in the driveway, rocking me back and forth slowly.

"It's going to be okay, Mary. You'll see. The Creator is with you, and He will not forsake you now in this moment. You must believe this."

"But, daddy, he thinks I cheated on him. He thinks I committed adultery," I sobbed and turned toward my dad. "I didn't, I didn't do anything."

"I know, Mary. We believe you. You're mother and I have prayed and we have peace from the Creator about this matter. We believe you," he said holding my face.

My mother called from the door, so my father helped me stand up. I looked one last time down the street where Joseph had taken off, but he wasn't there. My heart sank. He hadn't believed me. He loved me, but he hadn't believed me.

After I changed from my wet clothes, my parents sat down with my brother and sister and told them about what was happening. Amber cried so hard, and I couldn't do anything to comfort her. Colin thought it was the best thing that ever happened, instantly believing and asking me questions about the angel.

We all prayed together that night. We prayed for the Creator to protect the baby, help me in the days ahead, and for Joseph.

CHAPTER FOURTEEN

WHAT'S DONE IS DONE

I hadn't seen Joseph for two days. School was starting, and my parents thought as long as I concealed my pregnancy, going would be a good idea. It would give me something to preoccupy my mind. All I had done for the past two days was cry.

Every time I heard the door open, I thought it might be him. But as the hours ticked by, I knew waiting was in vain. The way Joseph had looked at me that night, I figured he'd never want to see me again. Worse yet, he could tell everyone that I had cheated on him and wound up pregnant.

I was sitting on my bed, when my mother came into the room with a letter in her hand. I knew immediately that something was wrong, but she handed it to me.

"It's from him," she whispered, turned and left.

Turning the envelope over, I saw that it was addressed to my parents. Slowly I took the letter out. There was only one page, and I recognized the handwriting.

Here's the truth,

I've tried. I've tried to think of every possibility as to how this occurred, but I cannot. I believed Mary to be a woman of virtue,

*and I trusted her...I loved her. There is nothing left to say, I must
do the right thing in the sight of the Creator. I will not expose
her sin in public, but I must break the vow. Consider this my
obligation according to the law as her agreement to annul our
union.*

Regretfully,
Joseph Abrams

My hands began to tremble, and every part of my body felt
cold. Rolling over on my bed, I took a hold of my pillow and
cried. Tears fell violently down my face, and I slid off the side
of my bed to the floor.

I looked up to the ceiling. "Why?' I cried. "How could you
let this happen?"

Sitting on the floor, I kept asking Him to help me. The
only thing that kept me sane in that moment was the truth. I
knew I hadn't been with anyone, and that the baby inside of me
was Divine. I couldn't see how this was going to work out, but
it had to.

I pulled the blanket from my bed and covered myself with
it. At least Joseph wasn't going to make my assumed mistake
a spectacle, but what would the elders say when he separated
from me? Unless he claimed it was his baby, everyone would
assume I had sinned. But how could I expect him to stand up
for me, when he himself believed I had cheated?

My sister came in and sat by me for awhile. I assumed
my mother had told her what the letter said, because she just
sat there rubbing my back. Amber was usually one to harass a
person mercilessly, but tonight she was a comfort.

She got my pillow down off the bed and lay next to me.
My bladder alerted me to the fact that I had fallen asleep, and I

found it endearing that she was still lying next to me. I sat up, and realized that my mother was asleep on my bed. My brother was in the sitting chair by the window with a blanket.

I laid my hand on my stomach.

"Your family loves you so much, baby," I whispered and made my way to the bathroom.

When I came out, I realized that I was hungry. Quietly, I stepped past my sister and went downstairs. I was surprised to see the light on. My dad was sitting on a stool up at the counter.

"Hey, dad," I said and tapped him on the arm.

He smiled, but it was a worried smile. I knew he was trying to put on a brave face for me, but he'd never been good at camouflaging his emotions.

"Mary," he said and went back to reading.

I took some orange juice and an apple out of the refrigerator, and sat down on the stool next to him.

"So, I guess you read the letter?" I asked and took a bite of my apple.

He nodded. "Yeah." He folded the paper and turned toward me. "You alright?"

Shrugging, I finished chewing my apple.

My dad got up and came back with a napkin. "You know your mother, sister, brother and I believe you?"

"I know," I said and took the napkin from him.

His expression changed and he sat down. "I've been sitting here thinking things over. Joseph isn't going to make a spectacle of things, but we need to make sure you and the child are fine. What do you think about going back out to Elizabeth's?"

I was shocked. "Are you serious?" I asked setting my apple down.

"Yes, Mary, your mom and I talked about it earlier. We want to make sure you and the baby are safe."

I took another drink of juice. Maybe he was right, but wouldn't that be like hiding? I had done nothing wrong, and it didn't seem right to run away.

"Then what?" I asked. "After the baby is born, am I supposed to stay hidden away and come back years later with an adopted little brother?"

He seemed to think about that for a moment. Frustration filled the air and he stood up and paced the floor.

"I've got to protect you though, Mary. This isn't going to sit well with so many people."

I laughed. "Dad, I think the prophecies spoke of the child being born to a virgin. Did anyone bother to consider what would happen if she told people?"

Shaking his head, he stopped pacing. "But this doesn't make sense, Mary. The Creator wouldn't put your life in danger, that would go against everything." He pointed down toward my stomach.

"Exactly," I agreed and bit my apple.

My father sat back down and turned to me. "Why are you so...mature about all this?" He smiled.

I shrugged. "I don't know if it's mature, or desperately relying on the Creator. Either way, things are somewhat out of my hands and have been for awhile." I yawned and my dad reached over and lovingly took my hand.

"Well, mature or not, you need to get some rest. Are you still planning on going to school in the morning? You know none of that matters anymore."

Standing up I walked to put my glass in the sink. "I'm

going. No one knows about the baby yet, and if Joseph doesn't say anything, then I should be okay."

I hugged him and headed back upstairs. With the rest of my family asleep in my room, I headed into Amber's room and got beneath the covers. I had to pee so much throughout the night, and I didn't want to risk waking them up. My heart was hurting, but I had to believe that somehow this would all work out.

Morning came way too fast. I was tired, but determined to go to school. The weather was beautiful, and I decided that a walk would do me some good. My mother protested, but it wound up being the easier answer for me getting to school. I assured her how I had walked every day while at Elizabeth's, and that exercise did make me feel better.

She finally consented, but wanted me to call her if I got there and wanted to come home. I agreed, knowing that I wouldn't call, and headed out the door.

Even though it was hot, the breeze was amazing. I made sure to tie a slim jacket around my waist to wear during school, and the shirt I had on gave no inclination that I was pregnant.

A few cars passed by me on the way to school, and I waved to a couple of neighbors who were out watering their yards. If not for my little secret, this would have been a perfect day. A few times I thought I saw a blue truck in the distance and my heart raced, but it was never Joseph. I wondered what he was doing.

This couldn't have been an easy decision for him. I felt compelled to find him and apologize, but what would I be apologizing for? I hadn't done anything wrong, but it felt like the whole world was crashing in on me.

The night he had pulled off in the rain was the night I

realized how much I liked him. I had begun to make up this story in my head about him and I being together. I imagined Joseph being there when my baby was born. Above everything else, that was a frightening part of this story. After watching Elizabeth give birth to baby John, I was a bit intimidated.

I made it to school only a few minutes later than usual. I stopped in the office to call my mom and let her know I had made it there. Turning from the office, I was met with squeals from my friend, Dianna.

"Mary!" She yelled and ran toward me. "How are you?"

"I'm good," I answered.

She pulled back and looked me over. For some reason I got a weird feeling in the pit of my stomach.

"Are you excited about this semester? I guess it's your last one."

"Yeah," I answered, realizing I would have the baby as the semester ended.

Dianna put her arm through mine as we began to walk down the hall.

"Have you seen Flower yet?" She asked.

"No, I just got back a month ago, and I've been at the mill most of the time helping my parents."

"Oh," she said with a suspicious look on her face. "And what about your man?"

I wasn't prepared to answer any questions about Joseph. "What about him," I asked.

She let go of my arm and stood in front of me. "Mary Lynn Meir, are you not going to tell me what's going on?"

It was obvious that she knew something, but I had to make sure of what the something was before I started talking.

"There's a lot going on, Dianna. You'll have to be more specific."

Even though she was annoyed, she wasn't close to being done with her questions.

"Okay, let's start with this. Why do I have to hear from Mrs. Levitt's, daughter's dog walker, that your neighbor Mrs. Bandy saw a huge altercation outside your house two nights ago? An altercation that left you lying in the rain being consoled by your father?"

It was actually relieving to hear that's what she was referring to. I started to walk so she'd follow me to a quieter hallway.

Pulling her aside, I whispered, "It's not that easy a thing to talk about. Joseph and I aren't speaking right now. I know you love me, Dianna, but things are just really crazy. If anyone asks, can you just not make a big deal about it?"

"Oh, of course, Mary. I didn't mean to seem like a jerk, we've just been really worried about you since we heard."

"When did you hear about it?" I asked looking around. Perhaps it was my imagination, but it seemed like people walking by were more interested in me more than usual.

"Well, last night there was a back-to-school rally on campus. Everyone was there from last year except you and Rebecca. Everyone knew about her quickie engagement last week, and we'd heard that she wasn't coming back to school. But nobody knew what was going on with you, until Susan, the girl who walks Mrs. Levitt's dogs, mentioned what had happened."

I was shocked. "So seriously, who all heard this story?"

Dianna looked around. "Sorry, Mary. It's probably the number one back to school topic. Everyone was already talking about how weird some of the believers were to get married young, and then some figured this kind of stuff happened a lot."

Leaning against a locker, I adjusted my jacket. I couldn't believe everyone knew about the scene outside of my house, but like I said before, this community was infamous for how they gossiped.

"So, where's Flower?" I asked. "Was she there?"

"No," Dianna answered shaking her head. "Thank the Creator for that. She'd have beat up anyone who said anything about you. Flower has never been known to be calm in a situation like that."

"Did you see her this morning?"

Dianna shook her head. "No, not yet."

We both looked around. It was now very obvious that people were openly talking about me.

"Well," I said with a sigh. "It can't get any worse."

"Mary, things can always get worse," Dianna corrected me as Kim, Katherine and Katrina headed our direction.

Not one for too much drama, I grabbed Dianna's hand and began to walk toward the gym. When people arrived early for school, they usually congregated there. I figured we could get lost in the crowd.

There were at least a hundred people in the gym when we entered. We usually sat at the top of the bleachers until the bell rang, but today I steered Dianna toward one of the lower seats. I figured it would be better not to isolate to a corner.

About a minute later, I felt more relaxed, and looked around. I couldn't see the three of them anywhere, but we did see one bouncing smile come our direction.

"Hey, Flower!" I called out to her and waved.

She waved back and made her way through the sea of

people. Always in a constant state of bloom, Flower was decked out in a colorful outfit that looked as if she was dancing.

"Hey, ladies," she greeted us and I stood up. "Mary, I'm so glad you're back," she said and gave me a huge hug.

"I'm glad to be back," I said looking around. "Have you seen the three K's?"

Flower laughed. "The KKK's are over there." She pointed. "I stuck my tongue out at Kim as soon as I came in."

Dianna laughed. "Why do you egg them on, Flower?"

She rolled her eyes at Dianna. "Why do you tolerate them?"

Dianna looked down and then over at me. "Well, there's a bit of gossip going around about our girl, Mary, so we've got to play referees at some point I'm sure."

Flower was the one to laugh this time. "What? Is this about Mary and Joseph's lover's quarrel?"

I gasp. "How did you know?" I asked.

"Ha, I didn't." She sat down on the bleacher and I sat next to her. Dianna stood in front of us listening.

"You see, Mary," Flower continued. "A lover's quarrel is always the next phase. First you get engaged, fall in love, or vice versa. Then at some point, the passion boils to the point of..." She jumped up and pointed her finger up toward the ceiling. "Drama!" She said it so loudly, several people turned, some laughing, some just shaking their heads.

Dianna pulled her extended arm down from the air. "So you didn't know anything about it at all?"

Flower leaned closer to her. "Well, okay, I may have exaggerated a little. I found it posted on someone's blog this morning, but it was the next consequence of being young and in love."

At those words I felt my face flush and the pieces of my heart crumbled even more. They had no idea that this wasn't just some simple argument. Joseph had officially in writing given up his rights to be my husband.

The baby stirred and before I realized it, I touched my stomach. Dianna noticed.

"Upset stomach?" She asked. "It'll be okay, Mary. I'm sure Joseph will come to his senses soon enough."

My stomach made a loud gurgling noise and they both looked at me. I tried to cover.

"Too much sugar this morning," I admitted, hoping that would make some sense.

Flower looked at me. "Uh, okay." She glanced over at Dianna. "Anyway, I figured the KKK would give Mary some grief today, so I came prepared." She reached in her backpack and pulled out a list. "Here, ladies, is a list of the secret offenses of the three K's, completely blackmailed from past boyfriends, employers and children they have babysat." I laughed. Only Flower could pull off something like that.

The first bell of the day rang and we headed to our classes. My first one was nearly at the back of the school, so I pushed my way past several bystanders in the hall. Even though school was really of no consequence to me anymore, I hated to be late.

I had slipped on my jacket as I made my way, and aside from my obvious reason, it was actually cold back here. I made it to my class just as the second bell rang and grabbed a seat in the middle of the schoolroom.

The teacher had started handing out class instruction sheets, when who but Katrina and Katherine came walking into the class. I wanted to crawl under the table. They looked directly at me, and I stared back, by no means showing any cowardice.

Katrina actually sat down in the seat next to me, and Katherine sat down behind me.

"Hey, gypsy," Katherine whispered from behind me.

I ignored her, but Katrina made sure to snicker loud enough so I'd know she heard her. Our teacher, oblivious to their petty teasing, kept talking. The person in front of me handed me a stack of paper, and without looking I passed it back to Katherine. When I felt she had them in her hand, I let go and faced forward.

"Way to go klutz," she said loud enough for the whole room to hear. I turned to see the papers all over the floor.

"Katherine, stop talking and pick them up," my teacher said, having apparently seen the exchange.

Obnoxious would define Katherine. "I'm not picking them up," she said defiantly. "She dropped them. Tell her to pick them up."

Snickers erupted in the class. Instead of a class of sixteen and seventeen year olds, you would think this was junior high all over again.

"Pick them up," my teacher restated, this time a little firmer.

Katherine conceded, but not until she made another nasty comment.

"Whatever you touch seems to get trashed, Mary. You might want to get that checked."

Katrina howled with laughter.

I suppose I got annoyed. I turned around and looked her in her face. "The only thing that needs to get checked is your attitude, Katherine. What's your problem?"

She tossed the papers in my face and stood up.

"You're my problem," she stated getting in my face.

Our teacher came down the aisle. "Ms. Caesar, if you have a problem, take it to the office."

A couple of guys in our class started saying the words, "chick fight," over and over again. Our teacher yelled at the top of her lungs for them to be quiet, and for some reason Katherine took it as a cue to back down. I stared at her as she snatched up her books and moved seats.

Forty-five ridiculous minutes later the bell rang. I gathered my things and headed out the door before the two of them left their seats. I wasn't going to hide, but I didn't want to put the baby in harms way either. Even though I had to pee, I headed early to my next class.

Dianna was in the next hour with me, so I told her about the drama from the hour before. Of course at the end of that hour, I rushed to the bathroom, surprised I could hold it that long. As I buttoned my pants in the stall, I heard two girls talking.

"So what did she say?" One of them asked the other.

The girl laughed. "It was priceless. She told her the only thing that needed to be checked was her attitude. Then everyone said she spit in her face."

"What?" The other girl gasped. "I thought Mary was a little nerd, but wow. You go girl!"

They left the bathroom and I was mortified. As nice as it was that people were on my side, so to speak, adding that I had spit in Katherine's face would only add fuel to the fire.

CHAPTER FIFTEEN

VISITATION

B Y lunchtime I felt ravished. It took a few minutes to get through lines, but finally I had a huge plate of food. I saw Dianna and Flower at our usual table so I headed over.

The lunchroom was crowded, and we'd even complained last year about it being like the streets of New York City. I felt myself torn between protecting my food, because I was so hungry, and keeping one hand over my stomach. People kept bumping slightly into me, but I kept focus on my destination.

About ten feet from the table, I saw Flower look and smile, but then her face made a crazy contortion and she rose from her seat. Out of the corner of my eye, I saw a flash of something dark and turned my head out of its way. The sudden movement made me a little off balance, and I found myself tilting funny off to the side.

I was falling, but the weird part, is that it felt like someone was holding me and I was gently laid on the floor. Letting go of my tray, I instinctively placed one hand out to the side and the other over my belly.

I fell to the floor in a sit, but it didn't hurt by any means. I immediately looked up to see Katherine recovering from the impromptu punch that she had tried to land earlier. I watched as invisible hands seem to turn her the other direction, and she all but flew over a chair that was to the side of her.

Flower was instantly kneeling, asking me if I was okay, and then I saw Dianna's face. She hadn't seen exactly what happened, and looked very confused as she looked over to Katherine on the floor.

Some people just looked down at me and walked by, while others, who had seen what happened, reacted with loud comments.

"Mary," Flower extended her hand to help me up. "Are you alright?"

I didn't have time to respond. A loud nasally voice rang out above us.

"What's wrong, gypsy? Cat got your tongue?" It was none other than Kim. "Oh wait, I think we should ask you a different question." Her face was fuming.

Flower helped me stand up and looked at Kim. "And what would that question be, Kim?"

Kim stepped closer to me. She looked me up and down and then talked even louder.

"Sorry I was late to school today, kids. I had a little errand to run. Seems I had to go buy a friend something." With that she took something out of her purse.

I stood there wondering what in the world was she talking about. Flower laughed. "We all know you don't have any friends," she responded.

Kim smirked. "You're one to talk, Flower. It seems the friends you do claim to have, are not the sort to be associated with."

Flower got closer to her face. "You've got no room to talk, Kim. Shall we bring up what you did over the summer?

At that Kim's face flashed a little concern, but she looked at me instead.

"I think we should ask Mary what she's been doing all summer. Apparently more than she's led on all this time."

My stomach began to churn. This didn't sound at all like it was going in the right direction.

Dianna stepped up and spoke. "Nobody cares about a stupid fight between her and her fiancé, Kim. We all already know about it, that's old news and no big deal anyway." She looked around as fellow students nodded in agreement.

Kim laughed. "Oh, I wasn't talking about a little argument. Here you go, Mary." With that she opened her hand and handed me a pacifier. I felt like I was going to puke.

Flower looked down at the pacifier and laughed. "What does that mean? The only people here who act like babies are you and your little followers." She pointed over to Katherine, who had finally made it to standing. Katrina was standing next to her with a smirk on her face.

I started shaking and felt like I was going to pass out. My heart raced around in my chest and began to hurt. I wanted to say something, but what could I say?

Kim stepped back further and made sure to captivate everyone's attention by standing up on the chair that was next to her.

"Gather round folks, we're going to play a game. Anyone want to guess the name of Mary's baby?"

At the mention of the word baby, several gasp could be heard echoing around the room. Flower rolled her eyes and looked at me, and I knew my expression communicated more than any words I could have said. She looked dumbfounded, and then looked over to Dianna. Dianna looked like she was about to cry.

Kim got louder. "Yes, it's true. Our little Ms. Perfect is going to have a little baby. My mom's friend is a nurse at county, and she shared the happy news with us at dinner last night."

I started trembling all over. This wasn't supposed to happen like this. But what was I going to say? I couldn't deny that my son existed, any more than I could deny the prophecies themselves.

"Alright," Kim said. "Come on now. Do we have any takers? Anyone have any questions or observations?"

A loud voice rang out above the crowd. Everyone turned.

"If you have any observations, you're welcome to share them with me. But my wife and child are of no concern to anyone in this room."

Mesmerizing. His voice was flat out mesmerizing. Joseph made his way through the crowd, while he kept his eyes on her the entire time. She got down off the chair and looked like she'd been caught at a crime scene.

My legs felt like jelly and I could hardly stand. I had to be dreaming. Tears streamed down my face, and Joseph turned from staring at Kim to me.

"Mary," he said so sweetly, but loud enough for everyone to hear. "I've come to take you and the baby home. I set up the crib in the extra room, and your mom and I were wondering what color you wanted it painted."

I bust out laughing. There was nothing else that I could even comprehend to do. Joseph grabbed my hand and led me out of the room. We went by the office, where I found my mother signing forms.

"Mom?" I questioned through my tears.

She smiled. "Everything's alright, Mary. I'm just signing some releases for the nurse in case you want to return to school."

I was completely awestruck. Joseph kept rubbing my fingers as he held my hand, and I seriously thought I had to be dreaming. But when I looked up to his face, his eyes spoke a reality that compelled me to believe this moment was very real.

When we got outside, my mother hugged me and I noticed our car.

"I'm going to go grocery shopping, sweetie. Joseph will take you...well, he'll take you either to our house or yours. Whatever you decide is fine with us. I love you, Mary."

She turned quickly so I wouldn't see her tears, but I distinctly saw her wipe her face as she got behind the steering wheel.

Joseph didn't say a word. He stood there holding the door to his truck open, so I hopped in and he came around and got in the driver's seat. A moment later we were flying down the road, but we passed my street and continued. I didn't bother asking him where we were going.

He drove for about ten minutes, and I realized we were headed to the lake. A moment later we were off the pavement on the familiar gravel road. Joseph pulled the truck into a shading parking spot beneath a huge tree in front of the lake.

I looked at him the entire ride. His face looked different somehow, and though he never looked my direction one time, I felt at peace. He had called me his wife, and the baby our child. Why had he done that?

After turning off the truck, Joseph sat there staring out at the lake. Without a word he got out and came around to the passenger side and opened the door. Instead of waiting for me to get out, Joseph picked me up out of the truck, kicked the door shut and kept walking.

I put my hands up around his neck as he continued going

further and further beneath the crowded tree line. After a moment he stopped and set me down on my feet. Joseph then held my face in both of his hands.

"Mary," he said softly, it was as if the wind spoke my name.

I guess I was in shock, but I didn't even feel like I had legs attached to my body. All of a sudden I sank down into his arms and he sat down with me in his embrace.

"I'm so sorry, Mary," he began. "I didn't believe you. I didn't believe you and you were telling me the truth. I am so sorry," he apologized again and caressed my face.

The wind blew around us as he looked into my eyes. He then looked down at my stomach, and a huge smile spread across his face.

"The angel came to me last night in my dreams, Mary. He told me about your son, our son. I will raise him as if he is my own. I'm sorry for what I put you through, and if it takes me the rest of my life, I'll spend every day proving that to you."

He hugged me to him and I held on. It was then that I started to cry. This moment was real. Joseph was going to stay with me, not throw me away. The Creator had been faithful and sent an angel to tell Joseph the truth. My heart poured out thankfulness to the Lord, and I knew from this moment on, even though the road was a crazy one, at least I truly wouldn't be alone.

After a few minutes I stopped crying, and Joseph leaned back, wiping my face with his shirt.

"Are you feeling okay?" He asked lovingly.

I nodded and found my voice. "I am now," I confessed and picked up his hand and realized he was wearing a ring on his left hand. He noticed.

"According to the law, I became your husband and you

became my wife on the day the elders met at your house and your father declared it. We'll still go through with the wedding, if you want to, whenever you want to."

I blushed and he answered my next question without me having to ask it aloud.

He whispered close to my ear. "It's going to be okay, Mary. The new house is finished enough for us to stay there, and I'll be sleeping where I usually do...on the couch."

Looking him in the face after that was near impossible, but I lifted my chin and did my best as I spoke.

"Thank you, Joseph. Thank you for believing the words of the angel." I took his hand and laid it on my stomach. His expression was priceless. Our son stirred beneath his fingers, but not enough for him to feel it just yet.

Joseph smiled and looked into my eyes. "Mary?"

"Yes," I answered with a sigh of peace.

"It's all really true." Happiness melted off every syllable coming out his mouth. "This baby...he's the One sent from the Creator; the One sent to change the world."

I looked out across the lake and watched the wind blow ripples across the water. There was nothing else to say in the moment. Whatever happened now...happened.

* * * *

We all sat that night and decided that Joseph and I would move in together. In our community, we couldn't be seen as husband and wife, unless we lived at the same residence. Although our home was just about ready to move into, because I was only fifteen, everyone agreed that Joseph should move in with us.

It would have been weird, but at the current rate of speed

my life had taken on, this was just another milestone in the path the Creator had chosen to put us on. Although it was a bit mortifying to talk about, my dad and Joseph openly discussed how they would move the extra couch into my bedroom. I wanted to crawl under the table, when they mentioned it, but my mom brought some fresh baked cookies to the table and changed the subject.

The next day they sent out invitations for a party in honor of Joseph and I. Even though we were sure most of the town new about the baby by this morning, my parents decided it would be a good idea for Joseph to officially announce our little blessing. This way, no one could come later and have anything to say about it…at least not to our faces.

We planned to move into our new house on my birthday in November. People would have less to say if I was sixteen, and Joseph was turning twenty-one in January. Our age difference didn't matter to anyone in our culture, but the laws of the land were very particular about the age of marriage. As long as a girl was sixteen, and her parents consented, she was able to do as she pleased.

Joseph wasn't kidding when he talked about putting a crib up in our extra room. After the dream he'd had with the angel in it, he woke up in the wee hours of the morning and built a crib. That was the only reason he hadn't come to me earlier yesterday morning.

It was gorgeous. I was shocked that he was able to finish it, but he said it was as if someone downloaded the blueprints and instructions at the same time. He knew of course that it was going to be a boy, but wasn't sure if I wanted the room painted blue or not.

He took me to the hardware store, where despite a few odd

looks from the counter personnel, I chose a beautiful shade of blue. It reminded me of the sky of early morning, so it wasn't exactly a baby color so much as a beautiful color.

I thought it was cute, when Joseph brought over some of his things. I made room in my closet for his stuff, even cleared him some space on the floor for his huge boots. He didn't make a big fuss about anything, although he did say he'd be sure to build me my own shoe rack for all the shoes that I had lying around.

Our party was going to be next Saturday, so I had an entire week to decide what I would wear. I was around nineteen weeks now, and our baby was beginning to make himself a little more visible. It seemed like one night I went to bed with a little bump, only to wake up with a significantly larger one.

The first night Joseph slept in the house was a bit awkward, but every one really tried to make things seem normal. We had all finished dinner and everyone said goodnight and went to bed. Usually, Joseph and I would watch television for a couple of hours, and then he would leave and go home. Tonight after we watched a documentary on wales, I clicked off the television.

Joseph stood up and stretched, and actually went inside his pants pocket for his keys. When we both realized what he was doing, we laughed and I stood up to walk with him upstairs. I wasn't sure of what was proper or not proper, but I went into the bathroom to put on a nightgown my mom had brought me.

When I came out, Joseph smiled and took some things into the bathroom. I looked over toward my bedroom door and noticed he had closed it half way. I wasn't sure if we were supposed to leave it open or close it, and I was thankful for his compromise.

I got under my covers and lay down. My son rolled around,

seemingly doing a flip or something, and it made me laugh aloud. Joseph came out at that moment and tossed his dirty clothes in a basket by the door.

"What's so funny," he asked and walked over to me.

I took his hand. "Feel this," I said and waited to see his response. The baby kicked with a resounding thud.

"Whoa!" He exclaimed louder than he'd meant to, snatched his hand away and looked back toward the door. "Sorry," he whispered. "Does that hurt?"

I replaced his hand on my stomach. "No, silly." I giggled.

Joseph sat down next to me on the bed, and for the next five minutes we were delighted and entertained by the movements of the baby.

"What's it feel like?" He asked me.

Thinking for a moment, I came up with the best relative thing I could.

"You know when you've eaten too much food, and a huge gas bubble makes you feel a little uncomfortable?"

"Yeah," he said with a nod.

"Well, it feels like that, except add on someone thumping you with their finger in the stomach from the inside."

He thought about it for a moment. "That's...interesting." he ended up finishing.

I smiled and he stood up and leaned down.

"Goodnight, Mary." Joseph leaned down and kissed me on my forehead. His lips lingered gently for a moment and then he leaned up with a smile.

"Goodnight, Joseph," I replied and pulled the covers up.

Chapter Sixteen

Preparation

TWENTY weeks marked the halfway point of my pregnancy. I could still get away with not looking pregnant, if you didn't know me, but I no longer had to hide. I had decided to take a little break from school, just to get used to all the changes in the house. My parents agreed that there wasn't a point in me going at all, but I had to go back. It was the principle of the matter.

I kept hearing stories about the day Joseph went into the school. It warmed my heart that most of the stories made him out to be a knight in shining armor, but then there was the whole debate about when I got pregnant.

Most people believed it was Joseph's baby. So even though they felt I was too young, they respected our culture. Some people, on the other hand, seemed to be in an uproar about a fifteen-year-old girl being pregnant and married.

We had lived in this society by choice, but my family still held firm to the practices of the old country and our heritage. The people of my culture were so happy for Joseph and I, and throughout the week, gifts began to make their way to my family's home.

The day before the party my mom took me shopping. She

wanted to take me to a real nice maternity store in the mall, and I was really excited. After dropping off my other family members to the mill or school, we headed out.

It was a Friday morning, so most of the teenagers I knew would be in school. Even though I wasn't afraid any more of what people would say, it wasn't fun being the object of stares and sarcastic remarks.

We found the place easy enough, and my mother began to hold up things from the racks of clothes.

"Mary, this would look so darling on you," she said holding up a blue dress.

I shook my head. "I don't know if I want to wear something so long," I admitted. "I think it will make me look about ten years older."

She held it up and looked at it again. "Hmm, I guess I see your point. Do you want to just get a top and wear some jeans with it?"

"Maybe," I said picking out a pretty yellow top. "What about this?" I held it up. It was a yellow eyelet lace top with butterflies on it. It wasn't too girly, and I liked the way the sleeves would fit around my arms.

"I like it," she said and walked toward me. "Why don't we just pick out a couple of things for you to try on?"

I laughed. "Aww, do I have to try them on?" I complained in jest. "I don't have any kind of patience."

She picked up another top. "Mary, you're about to become a mother. Patience is going to be your best friend." My mother smiled and went to look at a rack of jeans.

Making my way to the other side of the store, I was just on the other side of a rack and heard someone talking.

"Freakin' gypsies," a woman mocked. "I don't mind that we have to put up with them, but they tend to stink up the place."

Another voice responded, "No kidding. They probably can't even afford it anyway."

My stomach tightened, and I felt condemnation roll across my spirit. Why did everything have to get ruined with words? Those people didn't even know us, and look at the mean stuff they said.

The first woman laughed. "What I don't get is why they're not exterminated already. Did you hear how Herod wants to move them all to camps? At least that would segregate them from decent people. Then I wouldn't care what they would do."

"Why are they so bent on these prophecies?" The other voice chimed in. "I mean they're basically anti-government. All those prophets were loons. Did you see where they rounded some of them up and put them in prison for speaking against the officials? I say if this so called new leader shows up, they should shoot him on site."

I gasped. Just at that moment one of them came around the tall rack of clothes in my direction. She had no choice but to see me, and the look on her face communicated her outrage. Not saying a word, I put down the shirt I had and went to my mom.

"Hey, mom," I whispered. "Let's just go somewhere else."

She looked at me with her eyebrows raised. "Why would we do that?"

I took the pants from her hand. "Because it's a good idea right now." The only thing I could do without speaking to get her attention was point to my belly. She immediately followed me out of the store.

We walked down the corridor for a moment, when she finally put her hand on my arm.

"What is it, Mary? Is something wrong with the baby?"

I started to cry. "You didn't hear what they said, mom," I wept.

"What, sweetie? What did they say?" she consoled me by rubbing my back.

"They said that he should be killed," I explained. "They said the new leader should be killed on site. Why would people say that about a baby? Why would anyone want to hurt my baby?"

My mother looked around and then hugged me to her.

"Honey, no one is going to hurt your baby." She pulled back and put one hand up to hold my face. "Many of the unbelievers think the new leader is a man who is going to come into the world and take over Herod's rule. They have no idea that the Creator is to come as a child."

I wiped my face and looked into her eyes. "They don't?" I asked feeling relieved.

She shook her head. "Nope." My mother smiled. "So don't worry. You and the baby will be just fine. The Creator has promised this little One would come, and He will see Him safely into this world."

Sighing I hugged her again and then started to walk. Up ahead was a frozen yogurt place and I felt an intense desire to stop.

"I'm feeling a frosty chocolate mocha moment, mom," I said and pointed.

"I couldn't agree more, my dear," she said excitedly, took my hand and pulled me in the direction.

I laughed. "I love you, mom."

"And I love you too, daughter dear. Now," she said as we reached the counter. "Let's see what sounds good."

We got our frozen yogurt and went for a stroll through the mall. After twenty minutes I felt at ease, and we went to a different maternity store. Completely opposite of the last place, the employees were very helpful. I found an amazing top that went with some jeans that my mother insisted on buying. She said eventually my old jeans wouldn't work at all. The stretchy material in the front of these jeans would make it more comfortable.

Content with my purchases, we walked back out to the car. The timing must have been orchestrated by the devil. There, walking toward us with a group of women was Katherine's mother.

There wasn't any way to avoid the group, and she made sure we realized she saw us. Not only was Katherine and that group a pain for teenagers to deal with, their mothers had always made issues with our parents.

Her voice was always so weird, when it hit your ears.

"Well, why am I not surprised to see you here?" Katherine's mom's name was Tina.

My mother linked her arm through mine and steered the other direction. I knew she wasn't intimidated, but Tina's husband was in the military. To cause trouble with them always led to something more.

Tina stopped walking and her group paused. "Abigail, are you just going to ignore that I'm speaking to you? I thought your group prided themselves on taking the moral high ground?" She asked sarcastically.

I knew she didn't want to, but my mother stopped walking. I heard a sigh escape her as she turned and answered her.

"Good morning, Tina. Blessings on you and your friends for a fine day," she said with a smile.

Tina scoffed. "Blessings?" She asked and rolled her eyes. "The way you talk has always been so cutely antiquated." She walked closer and then looked at me. "Katherine told me about your little stunt at school the other day. I expect with your hormones apparently raging, you lost your senses momentarily."

She looked at me waiting for an answer. When I didn't reply, it seemed to make her madder.

"Abigail," she said looking then at my mother. "I suggest you teach some of your manners to your daughter." Tina looked back toward me. "But then again, I suppose your idea of manners is lost on an apparently whorish child."

That did it. My mother let go of my arm, took a step in front of me and raised her hand.

"Tina, I've put up with mess from you for the past twenty years, but my daughter is not going to be subjected to your ignorant mouth. She is not, nor has she ever been a whore. That title seems to be reserved for your own daughter."

If she had slapped Tina at that moment, no one would have been surprised, but what my mother did next was worse. She stepped closer and said, "I pity you." She then turned, took my hand and we walked off.

Stunned is an interesting word. I'd known for years my mother had it in her, but I had no idea she would literally let it out. We got to the car and she unlocked the doors. I put my bag in the back and got into the passenger seat.

Not only did she leave the parking lot, she left with wheels blazing. My mother was seriously having a moment. I sat looking straight ahead, as she accelerated to an incredible speed. We were home in half the time it took us to get there.

We pulled into the driveway and she shut off the car. I

didn't expect her to say anything; at this point I didn't know what to expect.

"Mary," she began and turned to me. "I love you, and I'm sorry I lost my temper. I want you to know something though. No matter what anyone says or will ever say, you are a blessed child. The Creator has looked down on this family with such favor, and I'm not going to let anyone condemn you for this. You hold your head up high, and by the way, you were right. You do need to go back to school, if only for a little while. There is nothing to be ashamed of, and we're not hiding." With that said, she smiled, patted my hand and got out the car.

The rest of the day all she talked about was the party tomorrow. Her excitement bubbled over onto me, and I found myself nearly skipping around about it. After my sister and brother got home, she set us all to work cleaning the house spotless. By the time Joseph got there, he was pleasantly surprised.

"Wow," he said looking around the kitchen. My mother had so much food preparation going on, and my aunt was headed over to help get things started. They would cook most of the night tonight, and then from the morning on.

I took his arm. "Wait till you see what they're doing out back," I said and winked at my mom.

We headed toward the back yard and through the door. Joseph's laugh rang out loudly.

"You've got to be kidding me," he said with wonder.

My mom and her friends had decorated the entire back yard. There were signs, banners and more. Some had our names together on them. One of the coolest things though, which caught his attention immediately, was the mechanical bull that had been delivered.

I shook my head. "Mom said you guys always have to have

something to be competitive about at a party. So she had her cousin Hyrum go get one for tomorrow."

"Aw, yeah!" He exclaimed, unlinked my arm from his and trotted over. "This is the one that will buck you almost a mile. I love it." He turned around and smiled at me. "Your mom is the absolute coolest mom on the planet."

Later that night, it was hilarious to watch my dad, Joseph and my little brother, trying out the bull. No matter how many times they got thrown off of it, they got back on vowing to go further the next time. My sister, Amber, tried it once, but one good throw was enough for her.

I smiled later, when as we were getting ready for bed, I heard Joseph in the bathroom talking to himself about how he did one ride too many. I felt sorry for him, as I heard him toss and turn throughout the night, but I didn't dare mention that I noticed.

Joseph usually got up and left early in the morning every day. So I wasn't surprised to hear his footsteps as he left. I drifted back to sleep, but woke up when the lovely smell of cinnamon hit my nose.

I rolled over, tossing off my blanket, and put my robe on. After a quick trip to the bathroom, I headed downstairs to the glorious smells of food.

The first person I saw was my aunt Michelle. As soon as she saw me, she squealed and reached out her arms.

"Oh, Mary," she said giving me a huge hug. She then put her hands on my belly. "This must be a boy."

I looked startled from her face to my mother, who turned around abruptly. We hadn't told anyone about the prophecy being fulfilled.

"Why would you say that?" I asked with a smile.

My aunt looked at me like I'd asked an absurd question.
"Because of how high and round he seems." She smoothed her
hand across my stomach again and smiled. "Yes, he will be a
great big boy, a man's child for sure. Joseph will be so proud to
have a legacy on the first try."

I blushed and looked at my mother, who changed the
subject.

"Mary Lynn, you need to get some food in you. What do
you feel like eating this morning?"

The kitchen was full of amazing things, but the cinnamon
rolls were calling my name. I walked over and took a huge one
off the tray.

"This will do," I said practically singing.

My mother handed me a glass. "Well, at least drink some
milk with it."

I went to the refrigerator and took out the milk. There were
even more delicious things packed inside. Avoiding the tempta-
tion to dive into the cheesecake, I shut the door and sat down
with my cinnamon roll. It was beyond delicious.

The party was set to start at seven tonight, but my mom
suspected some people would show up earlier. Parties were a
rare occasion the past few years, so many distant relatives would
show up to have a chance to see people. In our case, they'd only
had a week's notice, but believers tended to act fast when an
opportunity to hang out presented itself. The phone had rung
so much this week my father took to unplugging it at night so
we could sleep.

My sister and friends were excited, because boys would
be there. As young ladies, they weren't allowed to date boys
because we had arranged marriages; however, that didn't stop
the flirting and giggling. My mother constantly got on Amber

to control herself, and though my sister tried, she tended to find herself the object of many boys' attention.

For some reason I never had the same problem. I didn't pay much attention to boys, and found my schooling and hobbies to be a distraction from what most teenage girls were into. I loved going to dance class, taking pictures and music. Even though the social aspects of school weren't my favorite, I absolutely loved learning new things.

One of my favorite subjects was geography. I loved the class in school, and would sometimes make up stories about traveling to new places. The furthest I had ever been was where my cousin Elizabeth lived, but I would love to go beyond that and see what exists.

I helped my mother and Aunt in the kitchen, until some of my other relatives showed up in the afternoon. I knew the party would go late into the night, so I took the opportunity to go and lay down for a few hours.

My dreams lately were full of reoccurring events. Sometimes I'd be walking along a dim lit path, always following a brighter light source ahead. But every time I'd reach out, thinking to touch it, it would go further.

The dream that was the most puzzling was the one about the birds. Every few nights I had a dream about these two doves that would fly high above the world, always in sight of one another. The second time around the earth, one of them would always fall to the ground with a wing broken.

The other dove would soar a moment longer, and then purposefully plunge to the earth at a fast rate of speed. Before the second dove would hit the ground, I'd always wake up breathing heavily with my mind racing, trying to comprehend the events.

This afternoon the dreams were somewhat combined. I was walking along a dim lit road, no shoes on my feet. My hair was strewn all over my head, and when I reached up, there was a wreath on my head, but it was thorny.

I pricked my finger and it bled, and out of the sky flew a dove. It landed in front of me on the ground, and I started to follow it toward the light. All of a sudden I couldn't go any further. Out of the sky another dove flew down, took the thorny wreath from my head and flew with it into the light.

"Mary?" I heard Joseph's voice.

I sat up startled. "What time is it?" I asked.

He smiled. "I didn't mean to startle you. It's around six. Your mom thought you'd want to get up and get ready."

The light from the sun had dimmed considerably though my curtain. I was surprised.

"What time is it again?" I asked

Joseph looked at me strangely. "I just told you, babe, it's six o'clock. Are you okay?"

I nodded as a huge yawn escaped my mouth.

He laughed. "You must have really been out." Reaching over hesitantly, he smoothed my hair out of my face. "How are you feeling? Are you hungry?"

I smiled at his silly question. "Of course I'm hungry," I reasoned. "I'm always hungry." Pointing down to my stomach, I then patted it.

Joseph smiled. "Then you're in for an awesome time tonight. I think your mom and her sisters cooked enough to feed an army. I'd guess there's more food now than at Thanksgiving."

"You haven't seen anything, yet," I cautioned him. "Wait until this baby is born. My mom's already got party ideas, and they go far beyond food and a bull ride."

He stood up. "Speaking of which, there are some guys already taking a beating from it. Your uncle Matt says he's next up, and I wouldn't miss that for the world."

Joseph helped me get up off the bed, and left so I could get dressed. It took me a little longer than usual, because I kept having to stop and pee. I wasn't sure what was going on, but lately I'd been using the bathroom three times an hour. My mom said it was because the baby had grown, but if I was only twenty weeks and it was this crazy, what would it be like in another month?

Chapter Seventeen

Party Patrol

B Y eight o'clock the party was already lively. There were at least a hundred people in and around my house. My dad had been smart enough to have some of my cousins control the parking along the street, and some people had to walk from half a block away.

The music was awesome. My family was full of musicians, so my parents invited anyone who could play to bring their instruments. While I was sleeping, Joseph and some others had constructed a makeshift stage, and they ran the electrical lines from the house.

Lanterns were hanging all along the tree line and on the fences. It took on a whole new life, when at ten o'clock, Joseph turned on a sparkle of colored lights that they'd hung in the trees. I couldn't have imagined a better, engagement slash we're sort of married party.

Some of my friends from school had come, and I was so pleased that Flower was there. She had never gotten a chance to meet Joseph, and was elated after the meeting.

"I liked him ever since that day at the school," she said. "Any man who will stand up for his woman in such a way is the most romantic guy in the world." Flower sighed and grabbed onto my arm.

Dianna, who had met Joseph before at a family function, commented. "I knew he was a good guy, but I never imagined he'd go all knight in shining armor. Everyone is still talking about it."

When she mentioned school, I frowned. "I bet it's one for the history books at school."

Flower laughed. "Who cares, Mary? You have an amazing life, and anyone who talks about it is just jealous. Look around," she said and pointed at people in the yard. "These people care about you and love you."

"Rebecca's not here though," Dianna stated matter of fact.

I shrugged. "Her and that Luke guy kind of stay to themselves."

Dianna leaned closer to whisper. "Did you know he's not really a believer after all?"

Shocked, I almost choked on my drink. "What?" I asked baffled.

She nodded. "Yeah. They said after her family really did some checking, he's not from our culture at all. Luke just said he was, because he wasn't sure if they'd let her marry him."

"Poor Rebecca," I said. "No wonder she hasn't been around."

Dianna looked over at Flower, and they exchanged a look that I knew meant something.

"What?" I asked. "What aren't you telling me?"

Flower took my hand. "Now don't freak out. Rebecca's family is totally fine with it, and we heard she's really happy."

"What?" I asked again, this time anxiously waiting her response.

She sighed. "He's in the militia."

It took me a moment to process what she had just said. How could Rebecca, whose family was one of the most prominent believing families in the county, marry someone in the militia?"

"But the militia harasses believers all the time. How in the world are her parents okay with that?"

Dianna answered. "You'd be fine with it too, if you found out his father is a high ranking officer, and they are loaded. Rebecca couldn't be more pleased."

I was frustrated. "So what about all that stuff she said about moving to some house they had to fix up?"

"Ha." Flower laughed. "That's the kicker. Rebecca really had no idea, when she got with him that he had money. He took it as a sign that she really loved him or something. It's all pretty sorted. Anyway, they moved two weeks ago to one of the military bases."

My heart sank. Rebecca was a completely different person now. I had tried over the past month to talk to her, but she was always too busy with Luke. At first I thought it would just take some time and things would be like before, but now I realized it was near impossible. Anyone who was part of the militia couldn't possibly be a friend to my family.

I rubbed my stomach and thought about my son. The government was his enemy. Anyone who was pro-government would never understand about my son.

"Mary?" Joseph's voice brought me out of my revelry. "Are you ready for the big announcement?" His smile was captivating.

"Yeah," I answered and smiled at my friends. "Time for the big announcement." I winked at them and hand in hand walked with Joseph over to the little stage.

My father signaled for the musicians to stop playing. He took the mic and started talking.

"I'm so thankful that each and every one of you came tonight," he said and reached for my mother. "Come, Abigail, stand by me."

Although she hated public attention, my mother confidently took my father's hand and stood by his side. The crowd cheered, and I could already tell that she was crying. With a smile, she bowed, thanking the crowd, and then turned to my father.

"Tonight," he continued. "We are here to celebrate the union of my daughter, Mary and my son-in-law, Joseph Abrams." The crowd went wild with yelling and cheering. "And now, I'm going to turn the mic over for their very special announcement."

My father was beaming with joy as he handed the mic to Joseph. Joseph had a hold of my hand and pulled me with him onto the stage. The crowd began to hoot and holler even louder, until finally Joseph raised his hand to signal for them to stop.

"Thank you," he began. "Thank you so much for your warm reception. Mary and I are truly humbled by the love that you all have shown us tonight." Joseph looked over at me and smiled. I kept my eyes on him, petrified to look out into the crowd.

"We will be having a formal ceremony soon, but in accordance to our customs, I announce this night as the husband of this amazing woman..."

His sentence was cut short by a commotion toward the back of the crowd, closer to the house. Within the crowd a sea of green began to form, and with horror I realized that the militia had come to pay us a visit.

Joseph's arm immediately tensed, and he pushed me behind him, as a group of them neared the stage.

"David Meir," a man stated loudly.

I glanced over to see my father step forward. "Yes?" He asked uneasily.

The man walked toward him and then looked at my mother. "Abigail Meir?"

At the mention of my mother's name, my father took a step forward, blocking the man from direct view of my mom.

"What do you want?" My father asked sternly.

Five more men in uniform came closer to the stage. Joseph pushed me further behind him, and I couldn't directly see my father anymore. I could see the backside of my mom, and I knew she was shaking.

The officer took another step forward. "We are here to investigate a formal complaint of assault on Mrs. Tina Caesar.

At the mention of Katherine's mother, I knew this was about the incident yesterday at the mall. It didn't surprise me at all that it escalated to this extent. The militia was known for carrying out the most absurd orders. I was quite sure Katherine's father had sent them here, and I was sure her mother made certain it was during our party.

My mother looked back at me and smiled. I knew she was trying to calm me, but I had no faith in a positive outcome. All I knew to do was pray. Pray that the Creator did something to make this all turn out alright.

From the audience, you could hear voices getting louder. Then someone flat out called them, 'satan's soldiers,' and then things just got out of hand. Before anyone could calm the situation, one of the partygoers threw something at one of the soldiers. Bedlam erupted thereafter.

The next thing I knew Joseph was shoving me across the back of the stage, deflecting things that were being thrown. My mother screamed, as a man in uniform reached out for her arm, only to have my father tackle him to the ground.

That was the last thing I saw before I was being pulled through the gate at the back of the fence, and guided into the darkness of the trees.

"Joseph!" I yelled at him, but he ignored me and kept going. "My parents, we have to go back and help my parents!"

He stopped and shook me by both my arms. "You and the baby are the only thing important right now. Hush or else they'll hear us and follow."

Wrapping his arm around my waist, he all but carried me through the dark area. Twigs and rocks moved beneath my feet, but Joseph kept me stable enough to keep walking. When we reached the end of the trees, He opened a gate that led to someone else's yard, and we made our way through.

The lights to this house were on, and we ran through the yard as fast as we could. Joseph knocked on the door lightly, and an elderly woman came to the door.

"Yes?" She asked, squinting from the lighted house into the darkness.

"Please let us in," Joseph explained. "The militia showed up at the Meir's house."

"Oh, my," she said unlocking the door. "Is everyone alright?"

Joseph pulled me in behind him, and she took one look at me and for some reason smiled "Oh, it is you," she said with such tenderness. "Come in, child." She took my hand and I allowed her to lead me to a living room.

I turned behind me to see Joseph putting out any lights

he could. He ran around the house as if he knew it, not asking where anything was. The lady led me to a couch.

"Here, sit down, Mary. Everything will be alright."

Puzzled I sat down, but asked, "How did you know my name? Do I know you?" I asked just as Joseph came into the room.

He answered, "This is Mrs. Horowitz. I've done a lot of work on her house over the years."

She nodded. "Yes, and he's told me all about you, dear." Mrs. Horowitz smiled and let go of my hand. "You really are a beauty too. How blessed is my little Joseph."

Joseph went to the window and looked out. We couldn't hear any police sirens, so we knew that things hadn't escalated further, but I couldn't imagine what had happened to my mother and father.

How was I supposed to just sit and wait? I wanted to do something, but what could I possibly do right now? I held my hand on my stomach and knew what was important, but my family being in danger was hard to process.

We waited over an hour in the dark. Joseph said, if they were looking for us, they'd have already come, and that he wanted to go check and see what had happened.

"No," I said, even though I knew it was inevitable. "Don't leave me here, Joseph."

He took my hand and squeezed it. "You're in good hands," he explained and looked over at Mrs. Horowitz. "I'll come back as soon as I know everything is okay."

The tears started to form and I grabbed tighter onto his hand. Shaking my head I stood up and embraced him.

"Joseph," I said. "If anything has happened to them..."

He hugged me tight and then let go. Without saying a

word, he turned and went out the front door, instead of the way we had come. I knew why. This way no one would track what direction he came back and it lead to me. A smoky smell waif into the house as the door shut. My imagination went wild.

It felt like forever, but in reality it was about ten minutes. Joseph and my mother came pulling up to Mrs. Horowitz's house in his truck. I ran out the door to meet them. My mother flew at me.

"Mary," she said and hugged me. "Oh, my precious girl, thank the Creator you are fine."

"Mom," I said weeping. "Are you alright? Where's dad? What happened?"

She smiled shaking her head. "It was the craziest thing, Mary. People were fighting and acting crazy, and then all of a sudden, a strong wind blew through the backyard, nearly toppling the stage and all the lights flew everywhere. A fire started on the roof from the lanterns that I had hung by the back door." She paused and turned to Joseph. My mother took his hand and mine and continued.

"Everyone became more worried about the fire, than the reason the militia showed up. All of us, believers and soldiers alike, began to put out the flames on the house and the yard."

I stood baffled as she explained what had happened. Questions started flying from my mind out my mouth.

"But what about Katherine's mom's accusation? Didn't they come to arrest you or something? And dad...I saw dad jump on that guy. He didn't get in trouble for that?" I asked astounded.

My mother shook her head joyfully back and forth with a smile. "That's what's so crazy about it. After the fire got under control, the lead officer in charge said all they were sent to do was question me. They didn't know why it had been at such a late hour. He took my statement and they left."

There was no sane reasoning behind what my mother was telling me. Not only had the militia not arrested my mother, they had helped put the fire out at my house. Strange wasn't even a close enough word to describe this; this...was a miracle.

A weird pain eased over me. It was sort of like a leg cramp. But instead of in my leg, I felt it in my lower abdomen. My mother noticed the change in my expression immediately.

"What's wrong?" She asked.

I shrugged and grabbed my stomach. "I don't know. I just feel weird or something."

Joseph put his arm around my waist to support me. "What do you mean by weird?"

The pain was gone now, and it was difficult to explain. "I'm not sure," I said and felt my stomach. "It sort of felt like a weird cramp."

My mom let go of my hand and motioned toward the truck. Looking at Joseph, she smiled her worried smile. I didn't miss it.

"Mom?" I asked. "What...what is it?"

Once again she smiled, but it was as fake as a plastic piece of fruit. "You just need to get your feet up, sweetheart. You've had a busy day today."

The ride home was a mere minute, and I was never happier to see my father, sister and brother. My uncle Matt and some relatives were still there, and everyone was cleaning up. I walked around the side of the house to get a better view at what happened, and was stunned by the massive amount of damage on the roof.

"Oh, wow," I said as we entered the back yard.

Joseph sighed. "It's not too bad. I can probably get most of that fixed with my crew in just a couple of days."

I noticed that a great deal of the darkness was near my bedroom window.

"Did it get in the house?" I asked, looking over at my father.

My dad made a gesture that was a cross between yes and no. "Some smoke and debris got in your room through the window, and the screen burned away, but it's not that bad. The smell is pretty strong though." He turned to Joseph. "I was just talking to Matt, and we think it's a good idea if you and Mary stayed at the new house for a couple of days. Just so we can air it out and get that heaviness of smoke gone. It's not good for her, in her condition, to be in that."

"That makes sense," Joseph replied and smiled at me.

I turned to my mother. "Is all the stuff in my room smoky? I won't have any clothes then?"

"The few days you're gone, we'll get them all washed and see what's good. For now, your cousin Rhoda said she could lend you some things. You two are about the same size."

I laughed. "Mom, cousin Rhoda is about sixty. I think I'll just wait until mine are washed. Or better yet, do we have a washer at the house?" I asked turning to Joseph.

He shook his head. "We have the pipes for a washer, but the only appliances are the fridge and stove."

"Oh, okay," I answered and turned back to my mom. "I'll just wait on them then."

My uncle Matt came over to our little group. He was so tall. Everyone always teased him about being a basketball player.

"Hey, guys. Well, it's not as bad as it looks. I'll come back over tomorrow with Michelle and a few others. We'll help wash the walls down and get that soot out of Mary's room and the hallway."

My dad smiled. "Thanks, Matt. I appreciate it."

"Anytime brother," Matt responded and gave my dad one of those man hugs. He then looked at Joseph. "I suppose your guys will make time for the roof repairs?"

"Yeah," Joseph answered. "I'll call the guys later and let them know what happened. We should be able to get it finished in a day or two. I'll know more when I can actually get up there in daylight and access it."

After making sure everyone was fine, Joseph and I headed to the truck to go spend the night at our new house. The decision seemed the most logical, but on the drive there, I realized this would be the first night that Joseph and I would be alone in a house.

Chapter Eighteen

Home Alone

I hadn't been to the house for a while. As we pulled up to the drive, I noticed that a street lamp had been installed, dispelling the darkness.

We got out the truck and headed to the door. Joseph had been quiet the entire ride over, and I figured he was thinking the same thing I was. Not that it was a sin or a crime to be alone, because we were technically married, but it was still weird.

I was very elated when he opened the door. The wood flooring had been installed, and there was a couch and side table in the living room. Joseph walked over and turned on a lamp, and I was happy to see that rugs were even down on the floor. One was in front of the couch, and when I looked the other direction, there was another one that was a runner down the hallway.

"I thought you'd like the rugs," he stated and turned on another light.

"Yeah," I said and walked further into the house. "They look nice. I love the flooring."

He smiled. "They did do an amazing job. A friend of mine did it at a fraction of the price."

I walked down the short hallway and found the kitchen. I

saw the stove and fridge that he had mentioned, but there was also a toaster and a couple of glasses and plates on the counter.

"Did you get these?" I asked picking up one of the glasses.

"They're just extra from my place. I thought to leave them here in case we came out for lunch or something. Hey, let me show you what I did with the nursery."

He took my hand and led me to the door, but it was closed.

"You're not going to carry me over this threshold too, are you?" I teased.

"No," he said and squeezed my hand. "I'm just giving it a pause for affect. Are you ready?"

"Absolutely," I said.

Joseph opened the door and clicked on the light. It was beyond cute. I wasn't sure if that was a word guys wanted associated with their hard work, but that room was seriously cute-ti-fied.

"Joseph..." I practically whispered. "It is so...so..."

"Cute, huh?" He asked with a smirk.

I nodded and walked toward the crib. I had seen it already, but he had sanded it down and stained it now, so it glistened beneath the light of the room. The walls were the blue that I had picked out at the hardware store, and he had trimmed the room accents in white. Tiny stars were painted on the walls, a detail that must have took hours.

"It's beautiful," I said and looked over at him. "I didn't know you were an artist as well."

He laughed. "Oh, I can't take credit for the stars. Your sister came over with a couple of her friends and did it."

I was stunned. "Amber did this?" I asked smoothing my hands over the wall.

"Yep, she even did that." He pointed and I followed his

finger to the ceiling. There was a drawing of a sun, moon and more stars, with lambs delicately drawn.

"No way," I said staring.

"One of her friends from the art school did those. Said if the baby had trouble sleeping, maybe he could count sheep."

Placing my hand to my chest, I took a deep breath. My stomach tightened a little, and that weird cramp came back. I winced.

"You okay?"

I laughed. "Do you know how many times people have asked me that since I've been pregnant?" I teased, but realized it was a valid question. I really felt uncomfortable.

"You look like something hurts you," he said concerned.

"I've just got that weird cramp again. What did my mother say to do?"

Joseph took my hand. "I believe she said you needed to rest and put your feet up."

He led me out of the room to the bedroom. The door was open and he clicked the light on. The room was really spacious, and as he had promised weeks ago, he'd put in a huge bed. My face lit on fire, when I saw it, but he acted like it was just another room.

"Here," he said letting go of my hand and going over to a dresser. "It seemed silly to me at the time, but your mom said to go ahead and get the bed put together. She thought you might need to rest some time if we came to visit." He turned and handed me a huge t-shirt. "I put a couple of my things in here, I guess you could sleep in this."

I took the t-shirt and smiled. "Thank you." I held up the shirt. "Thanks mom," I said and laughed. "She has always been a bit prophetic."

Joseph laughed and took out a pair of pants and a shirt. "The bathroom is of course right there. There's only one towel, but it's clean." He turned to leave the room, but turned back. "Oh, there's only water and some lunchmeat in the fridge. If that's not okay, I can always run to the store for you."

I shook my head. "No, I'm fine. I might need some water though."

Joseph held up one finger and left the room. I held the shirt up to my face and inhaled. It smelled just like him.

"Here you go," he said, acting as if he didn't notice me sniffing his shirt.

Red faced I took the bottle of water.

He smiled. "I'll be out on the couch. If you need anything, just holler. Do you want the door open or shut?"

"Just leave it open," I answered. "I won't feel so alone."

Joseph stepped toward me. "You're never alone, Mary." He pointed to the baby. "He's always with you, and before He was, the Creator was always watching."

I knew what he meant, but I couldn't explain what I was trying to say. Without thinking I spoke.

"I guess I've just gotten used to you...being around...and stuff." I ended the sentence and a hot flood of embarrassment washed over me. But it was the truth. He was growing on me.

Sparing me further blushing, Joseph made a joke. "Well, I guess I'm getting used to you being around too. Even though I'm relieved tonight not to have to smell those awful pickles you eat."

I gasped. "You don't like my pickles?" I teased.

He shook his head. "It probably wouldn't be so bad, if it were one or two, but watching you, or rather smelling you eat down a whole jar...well, that's just gross, Mary."

"Whatever," I said, reaching over to the bed and grabbing a pillow. I aimed and threw it at him, but he deflected it. He walked over and retrieved it from the ground.

"Thanks, Mrs. Abrams. I needed a pillow." He turned and walked out the room.

I smiled and went into the bathroom. It had been freshly painted a mint green color, and the shower was enormous. Certain that there were no objections to a quick shower, I took off my clothes and hopped in. It was wonderful.

Twenty minutes later I was changed into the huge t-shirt, and snuggled beneath a beautiful quilt. I knew without asking that my mother had made it, and I wondered when she'd had the time. With all the craziness going on, plus stuff at the mill, it was a wonder she got anything else done.

Joseph peeked through the door. "Goodnight, Mary," he said and waved.

"Good night, Joseph," I answered and waved back.

He left the door wide open, and if I leaned up on the end of the bed, I could see down the hall to the living room. I couldn't see the couch, but I knew he was there and I was happy that he wasn't that far away.

I drifted off to sleep very happy and relieved. I couldn't believe the night had turned out okay, especially after the militia had showed up. I was still shocked by the amazing turn of events, and I knew people would talk about it for weeks, if not months to come. The militia had come to my house, and nobody was detained, arrested or beaten. I thanked the Creator with my last conscious thought.

* * * * *

There weren't any curtains in the room, so the early

morning light from the sun filled my room. I turned over in bed, completely happy and warm, delighted at such a good night's sleep. I hadn't even gotten up one time to pee, an event that I quickly jumped out of bed now to remedy.

I washed my face and came back out into my room, looking around in the daylight. The room was painted the same shade green as the bathroom, but in the daylight it was even nicer. There was a bed, dresser, a night table with a lamp, and a chest.

Walking over to the chest, I lifted the lid and peered inside. There wasn't anything in there, but I knew it was for storing bedding and things. My parents had one at the foot of their bed.

The t-shirt I had on was almost to my knees, so I thought it was modest enough to go see what Joseph was doing. I tiptoed down the hallway to the living room, but was surprised to find him gone. I went back toward the kitchen, and noticed through the window that his truck was gone.

I wasn't sure what time it was, but the sun had just come up, so it couldn't be too late. There was nothing to do but wait for him, so I decided to go out back to my gazebo. No one lived close enough to care what I was wearing, and it was so nice outside, I thought it would be great to go see the fountain.

The morning air was wonderful as I stepped out into it. The baby seemed to agree, as he gave me a resounding kick. I laughed and rubbed my stomach, wondering if he could feel my touch.

The fountain trickled water, and the sound was so peaceful. I absolutely loved my wedding present from Joseph. Every detail of this gazebo was so thoughtful, and I thanked the Creator that I had been blessed with a man so considerate.

I sat down on the bench and looked around. The area was

fairly wooded, and I barely noticed the fence that ran alongside the property. I wondered how far back it went. From where I sat, it seemed like there wasn't any fencing along the other side of the property, but I suspected it went further than I could see.

It wasn't the most elaborate property and house, but it was our land. I rubbed my stomach again and stared at it. This baby was going to help us protect the things that were rightfully ours, and one day we wouldn't have to live under so many restrictions.

I thought about what the woman had said in the maternity store. Some people were not going to accept my son as the Creator in the flesh, and I wasn't sure exactly why. Most of us imagined the Son would look different or be so different people would have to recognize His true identity and treasure Him.

"Mary?" I heard Joseph's call and saw him frantically run out the side door.

"I'm here," I replied and stood up.

Relief spread all over Joseph's face. "I came in and called to you, but you didn't answer. I couldn't see you out here from the window." He walked up and sighed.

"Sorry," I apologized. "I couldn't resist seeing my present again.

That made him smile. "I'm glad you liked it, but I nearly had a heart attack."

I smiled sweetly and looked up at him. "Forgive me?"

He smiled back. "Obviously," he said and laughed. He pointed to my stomach. "How's he doing?"

I rubbed my belly. "He is doing great." I walked toward the house. "However," I said with a laugh. "I'm a little hungry." Turning, I walked backward and looked at Joseph. "Do we have any pickles?"

Joseph laughed. "Why do you think I was gone? I ran to the store; they're in the kitchen."

"Yay," I squealed. I turned around and ran into the house, elated at the massive jar of pickles he had purchased.

Our breakfast consist of things that didn't need to be cooked. Although we had a stove, there weren't any pots or pans. I was content though. Joseph had brought fruits, cheese and bread. It was like having our own little picnic in the house.

He said he had called some guys on the construction crew, and they were headed over to my house to see what they could help with. After we got done eating, he suggested we go over and see how everyone was doing.

The only thing I had to wear was my clothes from last night. I went through the draws and found a smaller t-shirt that belonged to Joseph. I decided to wear that with my jeans.

When I came out the room, he looked pleased about my decision, and we headed over to my house. On the way over, he had some interesting questions.

"So, Mary, it dawned on me recently that we don't know some stuff about each other."

"That's probably right," I said and laughed. "I didn't even know your middle name until a couple of months ago."

He continued. "Well, you know all my names now, but do you know what my favorite name is?"

"You're favorite name? For what?" I turned and looked at him.

"I was going to be real cheesy and say my favorite name was Mary, but I'd be lying. My favorite name is Bob."

I cracked up. "Bob? What in the world are you talking about?"

He smiled. "Seriously, for some reason, when I was a kid, I

loved the name Bob. I named my first action figure, imaginary friend and dog...Bob."

"You had an imaginary friend?" I asked intrigued.

Joseph nodded. "Yep. He would get me in all sorts of trouble, but he was an excellent builder."

"I wonder why?" I laughed. "Well, I didn't have an imaginary friend, exactly. It was more like a frequent visitor, but it seemed to be in my mind."

He turned the corner and then looked at me. "Uh, is there something you're trying to tell me, Mary?" He asked sarcastically.

"I'm not nuts, silly. I just...well, sometimes it was as if I had this feeling that someone was around. It was only when I was little though. By the time I was ten I didn't notice it anymore, but it was pretty neat."

"Maybe it was an angel," he said. Joseph and I had never really talked about our experiences with the angel.

"Maybe," I replied. "I mean, I saw one in the greenhouse and talked to him. You had one come to you in a dream. I wonder if it was the same one."

He shrugged. "It's possible. All I know is after that dream, no one could convince me otherwise. I've never been more frightened and happy in my entire life."

"I can actually say I understand," I agreed.

We pulled up to my house and there were quite a few people around. I recognized my uncle Matt's truck, but the other vehicles were unfamiliar. I walked up the drive with Joseph, and he went to the backyard as I entered the kitchen door.

"Mom?" I called. The air still smelled like smoke in here.

She came into the room with a huge smile.

"Oh, Mary. Did you sleep okay?" She hugged me.

"Yes, it was nice. Thanks for suggesting he put the bed and stuff up."

My mother tapped her head and smiled. "On occasion the Creator puts some good ideas up in here. Are you hungry?

I shook my head. "We ate, but I'll take a piece of cinnamon roll if there's any left."

She opened the refrigerator and came back with a huge roll.

"Here you go, sweetheart. You want some milk with that?"

"No thanks. Is it alright if I go upstairs and see the damage?"

My mother laughed. "You know, it turned out not to be as bad as I thought. Another day and you'll be able to sleep here. It didn't get your clothing as bad as we thought either. I've got some of it washed in the laundry room, if you want to change," she said with a smirk.

"I'm fine," I assured her and left the kitchen.

My little brother was on the couch playing a video game. I said hello, but he just waved and continued playing. I went up the stairs and there were workmen in my room. I coughed a little from the concentration of the smoky smell. Peeking around the corner, I could see my aunt, Michelle, washing down the walls.

"Hey, Aunt Shelly," I said and she turned.

"Oh, hey, Mary. You shouldn't be up here yet, this stuff is still pretty potent."

Pulling my t-shirt up over my nose, I agreed. "Yeah, I know. Thanks for helping mom."

"No problem, honey. Now you get outside where the air is cleaner."

I waved again and went back down the stairs. My brother was still in the same spot, and I went out the door to the yard. There were workmen here and there, and I looked up at the house. Joseph was up on the roof, and some man was talking to him. When he saw me come out, he waved and continued talking.

The yard was a mess, and I saw a trash bag lying on the ground. I started to go around and pick up paper plates, cups and anything lying on the ground that I could. The stage had been taken down already, and there was little evidence of it.

The lights had all been unwound from the fence, and I walked over to pick up bits of debris. I still couldn't believe how the fire had started and everyone stopped fighting.

"You're home early," my sister's voice came from behind me.

"Hey, Amber," I replied and stood up. "I wanted to thank you."

She looked at me weird. "For what?" Amber was always very smart-alecky.

"For the baby's room, silly."

Amber looked toward the house nonchalantly. "Oh, that. It was cool."

I reached out and touched her arm. "I know all this has been really weird to have to deal with, and I know how people have said all kinds of stuff about our family. So for what it's worth, thanks for...well, you know."

Amber smiled for a moment and then went back to her sarcastic manner. "Like I had a choice. Besides, I'm all about causing a little controversy every now and then. Speaking of which, how was it being alone with Joseph last night?"

"Amber!" I hit her on the arm.

"Ow! What did you do that for? I was just curious. I know you're not living in sin or something, I just wondered if...you know."

"Amber Grace, I ought to..."

"Girls!" My mother shouted from the back porch.

She didn't have to say anymore, I realized we had gotten rather loud. Although the workers paid us no attention, some of the neighbor women were helping de-smoke the house.

My sister stuck her tongue out at me and I tossed a paper cup at her. She ran off toward the house and I continued to pick up the yard.

Every so often I took a break and went in the house to eat or use the bathroom, and it did seem that the smoke smell was going away. I took a pillow from the couch downstairs and lay out back on one of the benches. I fell asleep for a little while, and then went back to helping pick up the yard.

Joseph left a few times, checking on other job sites, and then finally returned around eight that night to eat dinner. We sat outdoors with my family for an hour or so, and when my father got home, he and Joseph talked for about the repairs.

Around ten, I started to fall asleep on my mother's shoulder. Joseph stood up and said it was time to get me home, so we bid every one goodnight and headed to the truck. My mom made sure to pack me some food to take, and I more than willingly took it.

On the way home, Joseph decided to ask questions again.

"So," he said with a smile in his voice. "Do you like dogs or cats?"

I thought about it. "Well, we've never had either. My mother isn't into the maintenance."

"Okay then. If you could have either one, which one do you prefer?"

Looking at the window, I thought about the dogs and cats I had encountered over the years.

"I suppose dogs would get my vote," I answered.

"Yes!" He exclaimed louder than he meant to. "Sorry." He laughed. "I'm just a fanatic about dogs, but was waiting to find the right one. I figure every kid needs a dog, so maybe we'll get him one, when he's around two or so."

"The baby?" I asked.

"Yeah, the baby." Joseph looked at me sideways and turned down our street. "Who did you think I was talking about?"

I smirked. "I don't know. It's just weird to talk about Him already being here; especially being two years old. Wow, that's just a trip." I rubbed my belly.

"I know," he said with a sigh. "But He is a kid. I figured He should do some normal kid stuff...right?"

"Yeah, I suppose." I thought for a moment. "I wonder what He'll be like. I mean, He's human, but He's so much more than human. He's the Son of the Creator."

Silence hit the cab of the truck the rest of the way home. We got out and went in, still quiet, and only after he turned on the living room light did Joseph speak.

"You know, Mary, all this is really weird." He sounded sort of sad.

"What's wrong, Joseph?" I asked and walked nearer to him.

He sighed. "It just really hit me, that's all. I mean, look at you...you're caring our Savior around in your stomach."

I looked down and smoothed my shirt down around him. "I know, and technically it's my uterus, Joseph," I responded trying to be funny.

Joseph looked at me like I'd lost my mind or he finally had. "How can you be so stinkin' calm about this?" He asked with a shaky laugh. "He's really here," he said pointing to my belly. "The Creator is here to help us, but more than that, He's growing inside of you."

At that moment the baby kicked so hard, my shirt actually moved.

"I think he heard you," I said astounded.

Joseph fell to his knees in front of me. "My Lord, how can I ever be worthy to raise such a child as this?"

I put my hands on top of his head and smoothed his hair.

"It's going to be okay, Joseph. The Creator will help us. We've been told the prophecies all our lives, and one thing is constant, He is faithful."

Joseph leaned forward and laid his head against my belly. He sighed and looked up at me as if a little boy.

"I love you, Mary."

"I know, Joseph. I love you too."

He stood and took my hand.

"Shall I escort you to your domicile?" He asked in jest.

"Why thank you, Mr. Abrams."

He walked me to my room and clicked the light on. Everything was of course just as I'd left it that morning. The t-shirt I'd slept in last night was laid on the pillow. I picked it up.

"Thanks for letting me borrow your shirt, and this one," I said pointing to the one I had on.

Joseph smiled, "You're more than welcome. Good night, Mary."

"Good night."

Chapter Nineteen

Time

JOSEPH and I were back at my house within a couple of days. I waited until then to attempt going to school. I was nervous, but no one really said anything to me. It was as if the subject wasn't as appealing anymore, and I was thankful to be able to continue learning.

After another month, it was quite noticeable that I was having a baby. Twenty-five weeks pregnant didn't afford any type of concealment. I was used to the stares, but was surprised that some girls flat out asked me about the baby.

Flower and Dianna were elated at my return to school. A lot of people had made bets that I would never return, and for the most part I received silent support in the smiles and nods from my classmates. I think Joseph's appearance at my school had actually done something amazing for my predicament.

But school was the least of my concerns. My brother had turned thirteen years old, and the military was considering advancing his mathematical studies. The idea of Colin having to help the military in any manner was disturbing, even more so, because of the baby I carried within me.

As with all things though, my family band together, refusing to let fear consume us. The government sent a representative to the house to discuss how amazing this opportunity was for my brother. Without overtly saying it, they implied that we really didn't have a choice in the matter. To disagree wouldn't have any impact.

Reports started circulating within our community about an increase in government raids on believers. While I didn't directly know anyone who was taken, more and more men around the age of thirty were detained. Some even seemed to disappear, with their families hoping for the best.

Every week I'd hear my mother and her friends whispering about the things that Herod had started doing. He was rounding up outspoken advocates of the prophecies. A trickle of fear went through me, when I heard he was seeking the whereabouts of the new leader. My family kept me comforted, with the knowledge that Herod didn't know the Creator would come as a baby. Nor did he even think it was our Lord incarnate; he merely thought it would be a man that tried to overtake the government.

Time seemed to speed up, and before I knew it, the calendar said November. This month on the 25th, I would turn sixteen years old. I had told my mother I didn't want to make a big deal of my birthday, because this year it was on Thanksgiving Day. I was content with having a huge cake at Thanksgiving dinner, and she seemed to be fine with that.

At eight months pregnant, everyone was getting real excited about the birth of my son. I didn't want to have a baby shower, but my mother insisted that it was a huge family tradition. She said this would be her first grandson, and that I had to consider what it meant to the entire family. I gave in, on one condition. It had to be a small group, and I wanted Dianna and Flower to attend.

Half way through the month, we got a suspicious note that was left on the door. It was around two in the afternoon, and I'd been left home alone. I heard a knock on the door, but when I went to answer it, no one was there.

The note was surprisingly addressed to me, but for some reason I was hesitant to open it, until my family got back. As soon as my mom had the groceries put up, I handed it to her.

"What's this?" She asked and looked at the note.

I shrugged. "Just something someone left on the door. I kind of had an uneasy feeling about it."

My mom opened the note and read:

Blessed are you, Mary, child of the Most High. There are some who know.
We are praying for you and the child. Blessed Be.

Instantly I lay my hand on my enormous belly. My mother looked up at me baffled, but a smile came to her face.

"Mary, we have to believe that others hear the Creator's voice and will know. This is a good thing," she said and held the note high. "People are interceding on your behalf."

I knew she was right, but it was weird to think that anyone knew about the baby. It made me feel vulnerable and uneasy.

"But if they know, what about the government? What if the government finds out about the baby, mom?" I asked trying not to sound worried.

She hugged me and then took my hand and walked me over to the kitchen table.

"Here," she said. "Sit down and I'll get you a glass of milk."

Always up for a glass of milk, I sat down and put my feet up on the other table chair.

My mother handed me the glass, and then walked over to the stove and turned it on.

"Honey, don't let this upset you. I think it's a good sign."

I sighed. "I guess so. It just makes me feel less safe or something. Like, wow, they know where we live."

My mother laughed. "Uh, Mary. You realize the only way they would know this, would be because the Creator told them, right?"

Drinking some milk, I thought about it and swallowed. "Yeah, I guess so. I guess you're right."

She walked over. "We will not give into fear, Mary. How can we? There is still so much we do not know, but we must believe you were chosen for this...created for this moment in time."

Her words washed over me with a confident peace. I rubbed my stomach and smiled. The child within me stirred and I smiled. "You know, little one," I said talking to him. "We have waited so long for you to come. Thank you, Holy Father for this gift."

* * * * *

The baby shower was on the Tuesday before Thanksgiving. Many of my relatives or friends were going to be out of town for the holiday, so my mom invited a group of about twenty.

I'd only been to one baby shower in my life, and was too young to remember what had gone on. My mother assured me that she and my aunt had been to plenty of them, and when I woke up that morning, everything looked beautiful.

The kitchen had been transformed into a beautiful landscape of color. Hues of blue were everywhere, accented with white and an amazing pearl color. They had hung everything that represented a baby on a cute little wreath, and it had white lights flashing off and on.

By noon, my house was full of women in varying ages. Dianna, Flower and another one of my friends from school was there. My sister had invited a couple of her friends too, and we all sat down to an amazing lunch.

Over in a corner, on a little table, gifts were piling up as each person entered the room. Some things weren't wrapped, and I saw a beautiful wooden plaque that someone had made for the baby. It was blue and white with a teddy bear on the front. The words said 'Baby's Room,' and it had a hook for you to hang it on the door.

For some reason seeing that made everything more real. I felt tears well up, but I stifled them down, not wanting to cause a scene. The last few months had been full of enough drama. I just wanted to get through this day peaceful and happy.

The cake was amazing. When they brought it out, the held-back tears poured from my eyes with joy. Every little detail was perfect, and I was grateful to be part of a family and network of friends, who loved me so much.

A loud knock on the door startled everyone.

"Oh, my goodness," my mother said with a laugh. "Sounds like the militia," she joked and went to open the door.

Imagine everyone's surprise, when we heard a loud male voice. It sounded angry or annoyed at the least, and I got up from my chair and walked toward the front door.

My mother was holding something in her hand, and yes, it was the militia at the front door. I could see past her to several of them along the sidewalk.

"Yes, I understand," she said to him, and looked at me with a weak smile.

The man walked off the porch, and I watched and realized there were at least fifty of them on the street. They seemed to be going door to door, and many of them had pieces of paper in their hands.

"What is it, mom?" I asked.

She sighed. "Oh, just another census taking place," she answered sounding aggravated. "Herod does this every so often, and then raises the taxes on our business and land."

I looked out on the street. "But why the big to do? Are there normally this many soldiers?"

My mother gazed out through the open door with me, and we saw other neighbors outside on their porches. The atmosphere felt alive with something I couldn't understand, but I knew there was something different about this census.

That night, after I went to bed, I awoke to the noise of loud voices. Joseph wasn't lying on the couch in my room, so I grabbed my robe and waddled downstairs to see what was going on. My father's voice was raised.

"This is an injustice!" He yelled. "I won't do it! I won't do it!"

"Shhhh, David, before you wake up the children," my mother pleaded.

Joseph's voice was calmer. "It was bound to happen, but I suspect the prophecies have something to do with this."

I walked into the room. "What's going on?" I asked alarmed. It had to be about two in the morning.

My mother sighed and walked up to me. "It's nothing really dear, just that silly census stuff."

"Silly?" My father sounded unlike himself. "With all the taxes we pay now, I can barely afford to keep a roof over our heads and the mill contract going."

Joseph stood up and offered me his chair. I walked over and sat down.

"So what's the deal?" I asked and tightened my robe belt.

Joseph looked down at me. "The deal is this: Herod wants every person to go the place their family originated from and register."

"You mean the census thing, right?" I asked.

He nodded. "Yeah. But usually when you do a census, you just fill out the paperwork and mail it in. They've even been done online. For some reason, Herod has required that we actually go to the original place."

I still didn't understand. "Well, ours is only the next city over, right dad?"

He looked even more enraged. "Ours is..." he began to reply, and then he paced back and forth. "Ours is, but you are Joseph's wife now, according to our laws and customs. Because we took the necessary steps to secure that, you will have to go with him to his place of origin."

Joseph looked sad, when I turned to him. I still didn't understand.

"Okay," I said innocently. "Then I'll just go with him."

The kitchen was quiet. I was obviously not getting some point that everyone else had processed.

Joseph took my hand. "Mary, the place that my family originates is over three thousand miles from here. It's on the opposite coast."

It took me a few seconds, and then realization washed over me. Three thousand miles was a long way for me to travel.

"But how would we get there?" I asked.

"Drive it in my truck," he answered and sat down across from me. "It's not going to be an easy ride, but I believe we can make out alright. I've got some money saved up from work, and we'll just have to do it."

My mother looked worried. "But how is she supposed to travel that far in her condition? So many things can happen when a woman reaches this stage of pregnancy. I'm just not okay with this, Joseph." I knew she was about to cry and so was I.

Always the optimist, my father embraced her. "Abigail, there is nothing we can do about it. You've read the notice. There is no way to get around it. Mary has to go with him."

She looked like she'd been slapped. "But they'd have to stop every so often, and that would take awhile for someone not pregnant. The only way for them to get there by the deadline is to leave within the week, David."

"I know, honey," he said and stroked her hair.

I tried to stand up, so Joseph extended his hand to help me up out the chair. Walking over to my mother, I smiled, but my heart was full of anxiety.

"Mom, it's going to be okay," I assured her.

"But what about your birthday, Mary? And it's Thanksgiving?"

I smiled. "It will be okay. We don't have to leave before Thanksgiving, do we?" I turned and looked at Joseph.

He squinted. "Hmm, I'll have to see. I think we could make it there in roughly two weeks. I don't know why we couldn't leave until the twenty-sixth."

Turning back to my mom, I squeezed her hand. "See, mom. That will give me time to celebrate my birthday with all of you, plus the holiday, and then we can go."

"Well," she said. "I guess if there's nothing that can be done, we must do as they say." Reaching over, she patted my stomach.

"It's cutting it close to the due date of this one, though," she stated. "What if you go into labor while you're away."

I backed away from her and laughed. "Mom, I've been looking like I was going to pop for at least six weeks now. Everything's going to be totally fine." I heard myself say those words aloud, and I hoped that I would come to believe them.

Joseph was eager to plan the trip. "Hey, David, if you will, let's go ahead and map out the trip. This way the girls will be more at ease. We'll time everything to be back by the middle of December. That's right before the baby is due."

My mom seemed happy with that. "I had all my babies at the due date or later. Mary will probably take after my side of the family," she said with a hopeful smile.

I went back to bed after thirty minutes of making sure my mom was fine, but I couldn't sleep. I'd only traveled as far as Elizabeth's place. I couldn't even imagine what it was like to go further than a few days bus ride.

The adventure of it was actually exciting, and I had been feeling really great lately. Except that I had this enormous belly, I hardly felt pregnant at all. I believed it to be a special grace from the Creator. Obviously He knew that this census was going to take place, and Joseph's family wasn't from around here.

Regardless of any concern or the fear that tried to seize me, I had to believe that all things were as they should be. I would travel with my husband to the place of his birth. I could do this. I had to do this. To endanger my son, by not complying with the rules, was not an option. I would trust our Lord to carry the baby and I safely through this journey.

For some reason, I thought about the note that had been left on the door. Right now, I was thankful that there were people praying for us. Mom was right; we needed all the interceding we could get.

CHAPTER TWENTY

BUMP IN THE ROAD

THE morning we left the air was clean and crisp. I was glad my mother had bought me a new jacket the week before. As we stood outside hugging everyone and saying goodbye, I had a really good feeling that things were going according to some plan I wasn't aware of yet.

Joseph had shown me on the map where we would stop that night to rest. I was glad he had been so thoughtful and meticulous about things. I felt safe and protected from anything that might unfold on the journey, and for the most part, I was excited.

I fell asleep about an hour into the drive, and woke up when I felt the movement of the truck stop.

"Hey, sleepy head," Joseph teased me.

"Where are we?" I asked.

He looked around. "Oh, about three hours in. You slept awhile."

I sat up and looked around. I didn't recognize this gas station.

"Well, that's cool," I said stretching my arms out in front of me. I need to go to the bathroom."

Joseph laughed. "Of course."

We went into the convenience store. It was around noon and it was packed with travelers. I figured many people were going back home after the holiday. A bathroom break and two chocolate candy bars later, we were back in the truck headed east.

I'd never been this way before, when I'd traveled to Elizabeth's house. The trees were beginning to look different, and I could see outlines of mountains in the distance. Another hour and I realized lunch was going to be necessary, so Joseph stopped off at a little diner at the next exit.

We sat down at the table and a waitress came to take our order.

"Hi, my name's Francis, and I'll be your waitress today," she said with a smile.

I smiled back. "Hi, Francis," I replied. "Do you all have pickles here?"

"The big kind or sliced?" She asked.

Joseph laughed. "Oh, she's talking about those big ones."

Francis nodded. "Yeah, we've got some of those on the counter. How many do you want?"

"I'll take one with our food, and then a couple for the road," I answered.

"Alright then," she said. "What can I get you two to eat?"

I ended up ordering a hamburger and fries, while Joseph ordered some type of barbecue sandwich. The food was so good, I ordered more fries and added a chocolate milkshake. Joseph sat laughing every now and then about how much food I could consume.

"It's not funny," I said with a smirk. "I'm as huge as a cow." I rubbed my belly.

He shook his head. "No, you're not. Honestly, sitting down

it's hard to tell you're even pregnant. Your face looks about the same, but your stomach is huge."

I feigned shock. "Are you trying to say I'm huge, Joseph Matthew Abrams?"

Joseph pretended to be serious. "No ma'am, but your stomach is. Speaking of which, how is He doing?"

Rubbing my stomach I smiled. "He's fine. Still moving around doing summersaults every now and then."

"How are your legs and stuff? Your mom was worried about your circulation. She sent me a text to remind me to stop every two hours so you could stretch your legs. Unless of course you're asleep, but I think it's a good idea."

I nodded. "That is a good idea. I did notice it felt good to get out just..."

A man appeared near our table. The reason I say appeared, was because we didn't see him walk up, and he stood there looking at me really weird.

"You need something?" Joseph asked defensively.

The man didn't answer, and a very weird feeling overtook me. He was dressed in shabby clothes, was dirty, and the smell emitting from him made me grab my napkin and stick it over my nose. Joseph stood up.

"Hey, buddy, is there something you need?" This time Joseph sounded flat out angry.

That seemed to get the man's attention more, but instead of answering Joseph, he looked down at me and smiled.

"May I have a drink of water, miss?" He asked looking at my cup.

I looked up at Joseph, who was about to come unglued. Just when he was about to say something to the man again, I interrupted.

"Wait," I said holding up my hand. I picked up my glass of water and handed it to the man. "Here you go," I said holding the glass closer to him.

"Bless you, child," he answered, and then walked away from the table.

Joseph stood for a moment watching him, and then sat down.

"What was that about?" He asked, still looking and sounding defensive.

I shrugged. "I don't know."

We finished our meal, grabbed my pickles to go, and headed out to the truck. The man was nowhere in sight, as Joseph looked around cautiously and helped me into the truck.

There wasn't any point in talking about it. Neither one of us had an answer for why that had happened, and why it had made us both react the way we did. We sat driving silently, and I eventually fell asleep.

The noise of thunder woke me, and I realized the windshield wipers were going back and forth quickly. Leaning up off of the side door, I turned to look at Joseph. He smiled at me and took my hand.

"How are we doing?" He asked looking down at my belly.

I rubbed it. "We are doing fine, but we may have to pee. What time is it?"

"You slept about three hours this time." He looked around. "This isn't the best place to stop. Do you think you'll be alright for about four more miles?"

"Uh...how long is four more miles?" I replied.

"About ten minutes, but if that's not okay, we can stop."

I looked out the window. It looked like we were in a small city, but the roads and buildings were old and falling apart.

"Where are we?" I asked squeezing his hand.

"I had to change the route because of construction. It's a little town that will take us about an hour off our time, but there was no other way to do it."

"So," I said, beginning to feel pressure on my bladder. "It would be a bad thing for me to say I can't hold it?" I looked over pleadingly, not quite sure I could hold it ten minutes.

Joseph sighed. "Well, in that case, stop it is." He turned down a street that led us to what looked like a store of some sort. After turning off the truck, he looked at me and then retrieved something from under the seat.

"Don't freak out," he said as he produced a small pouch. "Your dad gave this to me just in case we found ourselves in a weird area."

I watched as Joseph took out a gun!

"You're kidding me!" I exclaimed, immediately alarmed.

He took my hand. "Mary, it's not that big a deal. It's just for safety. I'm sure everything will be alright." With that said, he took the gun, put it in his jacket pocket and got out. All I could think was, 'Creator, be with us.'

Joseph held my hand as we walked from the truck to the door. The rain had made huge puddles, and my feet sank down in them about an inch wetting my sneakers. When we reached the door, it had huge metal bars down it, and didn't look like the most welcoming place.

It was open though, so we walked in and I saw a dimly lit room with a counter. We walked up to the counter to see a little old man wearing a dirty apron.

"Yes," was all he said, not even looking up.

Joseph answered. "Can we use your restrooms?"

The man didn't look up. "They're not free. You have to buy something."

We looked at each other and then around at the store. There were a couple of questionable food items, a coffee machine and some magazines.

"Okay," Joseph replied. "I'll buy a couple of those waters," he said pointing behind the man.

This time the man looked up. "That's not enough," he said without emotion and then went back to reading his paper.

I really had to go to the bathroom. I squeezed Joseph's hand and danced around for a moment to let him know. He noticed.

"Okay, sir. Can you tell me what I need to buy so she can use the restroom?"

Without looking up again the man answered. "You can buy something that cost twenty dollars. The bathroom is through there." He pointed through some dark hanging curtains.

There was no way I was going through those doors by myself. I looked up at Joseph and I knew he thought the same thing.

"Here, how about I give you twenty dollars, and we just go back there?" Joseph reached into his wallet, produced the twenty and handed it to the man.

The man put his paper down, took the twenty and then put a cigar in his mouth. He nodded toward the curtain as he struck a match to light his cigar. "Go ahead," he said.

Joseph took my hand and led me through the filthy, dark curtain. Just on the other side was a door to my left that said restroom. I opened the door, but Joseph peeked in and turned the light on for me.

"It's not the best, but it's okay, Mary," he said with an

encouraging smile. "Hover best you can," he advised with a wink.

I walked in and shut the door. Five difficult hovering moments later, I washed my hands and opened the door. Joseph grabbed my hand, before I could even say anything, and walked at a fast pace.

When we entered the other room, there were some men up at the counter talking. They all got quiet and stared at us, but Joseph kept walking until we were out the door.

The rain had picked up, and the puddles outside were even bigger than when we went inside. There was no way to avoid the plunge, so we set out the short distance to the truck.

The loud sound of a door slamming made me jump, and I turned around to see that a few of the men had come out behind us. They watched with eager eyes, and my stomach churned as I saw one of them come toward us.

Joseph opened the passenger side door and practically tossed me up onto the seat. He slammed the door behind himself, and stood with his back against the door. The rain was pouring down so hard it was difficult to make out what happened next.

From the far right side of the sidewalk, a figured appeared. All the other men turned that direction, and I saw Joseph duck. A fist crashed against my window with a thud, and I jumped in my seat realizing what was going on.

Still unable to see what was happening, I was tempted to open the door. Right at that moment the baby kicked me so hard, I was too distracted to follow through. Just then, the driver's side door opened, and Joseph hoped in and started the truck.

"Put your seatbelt on!" He yelled.

I complied as he put the truck in reverse and peeled

backward out of the parking space. He forced it quickly into drive and we sped down the road.

"What happened?" I asked, shocked to see blood on the side of Joseph's face.

He reached up and wiped it off a little. "I suspect they were going to try and rob us, but that guy came out of nowhere."

"What guy?" I asked.

Joseph almost cheered. "I don't know, but thank the Creator he did. He took the other three out before I could comprehend what was going on."

"Are you okay?" I asked reaching up with a napkin.

He took the napkin and dabbed his face. "Yeah, the guy didn't hit me. I actually hit my ear on the side mirror of the truck, when I ducked," he explained.

Tears welled up in my eyes. "I can't believe this," I said.

Joseph grabbed my hand. "Mary, we're okay. Everything is okay. I'm fine, you're fine, and most importantly, the baby is fine." He smiled and the reached out to touch my stomach.

I wiped the tears from my face. "I know," I offered. "But what if something had happened to you?"

"Nothing is going to happen to me, Mary. The Creator is watching over us and His will far outweighs anything someone could do."

Sighing, I wiped my face and placed my hand on his. Beneath our hands lay the most important person. I had to believe that the Creator would protect us, no matter what happened.

Joseph looked over at me and then back toward the road. "You know, you look absolutely beautiful."

I reached up and touched my wet hair and laughed. "Uh, okay, Joseph. So I guess you like the wet dog look?"

Without looking at me, he answered. "I love you, Mary. Everything's going to be okay. We're going to get to the other coast, register and be back home in a week or so."

As the rain pounded on the car window, I could only hope that what he was saying was true. It seemed simple in theory and plan, but after what had just happened, I wasn't so sure things would go according to Joseph's plan.

Chapter Twenty-One

Good Samaritan

THE weather was not cooperative. I called my parents a week into the journey, and they said the rain had also been an issue there. My brother and sister were doing well, but Colin had been invited to a military gathering. I knew my mother was frantic, but she tried to remain optimistic despite her fear.

The militia was making even more trouble. She said there had been a raid at the high school for some reason, with parents and students that were believers being harassed.

Flower's parents had actually taken her out of school, and she was going to stay with a cousin in the country. I knew my mother was holding back some information. For Flower's family to take her practically into hiding, something incredible must have happened. Whatever it was, I could only now pray for my friends and family.

Another two weeks passed, and due to the weather and construction work, we were getting days behind on our schedule. In the back of my mind I was beginning to be concerned about making it back in time, but Joseph was still confident that we would be okay.

It was now the seventeenth of December, and Joseph said we would reach the registration city in about a day. I was excited that our journey was halfway over, but couldn't fathom how we would make it back home by my due date.

When I talked to my mom about it, she was banking on a late arrival of the baby. She said most first time mothers usually went the entire forty weeks, if not more, so I was at ease that we would be safely home.

Finally, we made it to the largest city I had ever seen. There were tall buildings at home, but these buildings were double the size of any I had seen before. The place we needed to register was a suburb of this city, but we were tired and it was too late to reach it tonight.

It took Joseph two hours to find a cheap place for us to stay, and though it wasn't the best, it was all that was left. Because of the census, people had come from all over. The manager said we had one of the last rooms, but we could only have it for one night.

To say it was crowded would be an understatement. Joseph had to let me out at the door of the motel, and then walk back from parking about a mile away. I sat anxiously on the bed for him to return, and it did bring me some comfort that he had my dad's gun with him.

About thirty minutes later he returned, and had brought some food with him. It wasn't much, but it was enough for tonight and the morning. I scarfed down some rolls that he'd gotten, and then lay down.

Sleep wasn't an option. There were so many loud noises; cars, people and some things I couldn't distinguish. Joseph sat in a chair by the door, pretending as if it was more comfortable, but I knew he was watching the door.

There was a broken down looking radio on the side table, so I turned it on. I turned the channels one by one, but all that was on was news. Crime sprees, stuff about the government and more negative news filtered throughout the air of the room, until I just shut it off.

Joseph stood up and stretched. "You should try to sleep, Mary. We've got to be out of here early in the morning."

I yawned. "You mean early today," I said pointing to the clock. It was already four in the morning.

He yawned too. "Wow, it's already that late...or, I mean early?" Joseph smiled. I knew his little attempt at humor was to distract me from our obvious predicament.

I sat up. "What time do we need to be out?"

"Seven," he answered and yawned again.

"Well, if I can't sleep, why don't you try to?" I asked and scooted over on the bed.

He shook his head. "I couldn't sleep, Mary. It's a lot easier to bear having you in this situation, if I torture myself a little bit."

"Why would you say that?" I asked.

Joseph leaned back in the chair. "If you haven't notice, babe, we're in the middle of Gotham city or something. On my way back, I was hoping you and the baby weren't taken by the Joker."

"There wasn't anything we could do about it, Joseph. Herod ordered the census, and this is where your family is from. What else could we have done?"

The chair legs came down with a thud. "I realize that, Mary, but you shouldn't be here like this, nine months pregnant. This dump looks like it's about to fall down on top of us, the food is horrible, and you look exhausted."

I shrugged. "The food wasn't that bad, and I'm sure the

walls will hold for a few more hours. At least I got to put my legs up, and even if I didn't sleep, my body got a rest."

Joseph stood up and paced in front of the doorway. "I'm not even sure where we go from here, Mary. The city is so crowded, and I'm sure the suburbs are just as bad."

"The Creator will provide," I said trying to assure him.

He walked over and looked down at me. I loved the way Joseph looked at me. Never in my life had I ever had anyone's eyes reflect the depth of love I could see in him.

"Mary, I don't want anything to happen to you and Him," he said looking at my belly. "It's as if I was born for this one purpose, and if I fail, the consequences are more than we could possibly imagine.

I took his hand. "And our Creator knew that, Joseph. He knew the kind of man you would be, and that you would protect His Son, as if He were your own. I have faith in you, and I know you will do what is best. Don't be afraid...I'm not."

Joseph smiled. "How do you do that?" He asked.

"What?"

"Make me feel as if I can do anything...like I'm superman or something."

Wiggling toward the end of the bed, I used his arm as leverage to stand up. "But you are a super man, Joseph." I hugged him around the neck, and we both were startled by a resounding kick from within me.

"Whoa," Joseph said. "I actually felt that." He stared down amazed.

I laughed. "Well, I'm glad I could share that moment with you, but now I have to pee."

Waddling to the bathroom, I yawned, but I was content.

I figured after we registered tomorrow, we'd find a place to rest and then be on our way back home.

******

Trying to start the truck again, Joseph put his head down on the steering wheel.

"There is no way this is happening," he said and looked over at me. "I have no idea what's wrong."

We'd gotten up that morning intent on making it out of the city, when the truck had suddenly stopped working.

"Do we need to find a mechanic shop?" I offered, trying to help.

Joseph looked at me, trying not to be annoyed. "I thought about that obviously, but I have to find a place for you to stay while I look."

I sighed. "What if we ask about a repair place, and then I can just sit there with you? As long as my feet are up I feel fine, and I'd rather not be alone some place."

He thought about it for a moment. "I guess that sounds okay, but first we've got to locate a shop. Let's walk down there to that restaurant. You can order something, and I'll see if they have a phone book."

It took over thirty minutes for them to seat us in the crowded restaurant. My feet were aching badly, but we had a booth, so I was able to sit sideways. Joseph left to get a directory, and I ordered some milk. The waitress seemed annoyed that we didn't order any food, and after ten minutes of declining her offer to order more, she commented that we should find another place to just sit.

Joseph had found the necessary information he needed, so we left and headed down the street. Walking felt great, after being in the car for weeks or resting on terrible beds, so I was enjoying myself.

He decided to see if we could find a place to stay. Some of the hotels had signs indicating that they were owned by believers. We took it as a good sign, but every place we entered was either too full, or charged a ridiculous rate.

We stood in line at one place for ten minutes. When we walked up to the counter to inquire about a room, they told us there were none. I sat down in a chair, waiting for Joseph to make a phone call, and a couple came in and asked about a room. Without a pause, the personnel gave them a room. The rate was even less than they had quoted us.

When Joseph came back I told him, so he asked the man at the counter. The exchanged got heated in a moment, and I pulled on Joseph's arm to just walk away. He was obviously upset, because he expressed how due to my pregnancy, we needed a place for me to rest. The man didn't even care.

Joseph was mad as we left. "And they call themselves believers?" He seethed. "I wonder what they believe in?"

I held onto his arm. "The Creator will provide, Joseph. We have to believe." As we walked, I kept praying aloud in my heart.

Street vendors were everywhere, and if we'd had more money, I would have bought so many things for the baby. We went past a lady who was selling hand made blankets. I looked at all her items for babies, and they were gorgeous, but outrageously priced.

"See something you like?" She asked enthusiastically.

I smiled. "Oh, absolutely," I answered. "These are all so beautiful." I felt along the lines of a blanket. "How much is this?" I asked.

"Forty dollars," she answered and picked it up. "Do you want it?"

Shaking my head I thanked her. "Thanks, but I can't afford it. You do beautiful work though."

The woman smiled at me, and seemed to think for a moment and then said, "I'll give it to you for half. Twenty dollars and it's yours."

I looked over at Joseph, who reached into his pocket and produced a twenty dollar bill. I knew we didn't have many of those left, so I stopped him.

"It's okay," I said and looked at her. "Thank you, but we'll have to pass this time."

The woman looked shocked, and Joseph was about to insist, but I turned away from the table and walked toward another. Joseph was soon behind me.

"Why didn't you get it?" He asked and took my hand.

"Because we don't know how much the truck will cost."

He sighed. "I guess that is the responsible answer, but I know you really liked those blankets, Mary."

"I really like a lot of things, Joseph. Including riding in a truck, eating and sleeping in a bed." I squeezed his hand. "It's okay, really. Hey, isn't that the repair place across the street?" I asked and pointed the direction.

Joseph looked over and then down at a piece of paper he'd written the address on. "Yeah, that's it. Let's cross here."

We crossed the busy street and entered the shop. The man told Joseph they could tow the truck here and assess it, but even that was going to cost us about a hundred dollars. There wasn't anything to do but agree, and we sat in the shop waiting.

Joseph found a chair so I could put my feet up, and I soon

fell asleep to the sound of tools and vehicles being driven in and out.

"Mary?" Joseph's voice roused me.

"Yeah," I replied instantly aware of my surroundings.

"They got the truck here, and it's worse than I thought. The guy said they have to order in the part, but they'll try to get it here as soon as possible. It will take about four days to get the piece and a couple of days to put it in."

"But what are we going to do?" I asked with concern.

"That's the cool part," he responded and smiled. "This guy has a garage apartment upstairs. He said he would let us stay in his room in exchange for me working on this place. His roof is pretty messed up from a storm, and there's some dry walling that I can finish. He has all the tools I'll need, so it will work out."

Relieved, I had him help me take my legs off the chair and stand up. I yawned and he hugged me.

"I'm so sorry, Mary," he apologized. "Let's get you upstairs so you can lie down. I already went up there, it's actually a nice place."

"Where is he going to sleep?" I asked.

"On his couch. The bedroom door locks, so it's not like you'll be up there and have to worry. I won't be far at any time, and I'll come and check on you."

Of all the things that had and could happen, this really wasn't a bad deal. The room was neater than I had thought a mechanic would keep it, and the bonus was the shower. I hadn't had a decent shower in so long, and it felt good to let the hot water consume my body.

Over the next week, Joseph worked around the clock. The mechanic was really a nice guy, and we had a couple of nights all sitting together eating dinner. One night the conversation steered to the government, and we found out that our new friend was a believer.

His name was Mark. His family owned the business, but he and a cousin ran it. I could tell something was different about him, but I couldn't put my finger on it, until he felt comfortable enough to explain.

We stood around the kitchen preparing dinner, and I noticed a picture of a guy on the counter.

"Who is that?" I asked, handing Mark the salt.

A panicky look fell on his face, but he sighed and turned toward me.

"He's one of the reasons I stay away from the decent folks of society," he answered and stirred the meat around in the pan.

"I'm sorry," I apologized. "I didn't mean to be weird or something. He's a nice looking guy."

Mark laughed. "Yeah, that's the problem. He was my nice-looking boyfriend for about five years."

Joseph, who had been sitting at the table reading, cleared his throat.

"You know, Mark. I don't know if you've heard, boyfriends aren't cool with believers." His voice was over the top sarcastic, and Mark and I both turned to look at him as he continued.

Joseph closed his book and looked at us. "We are not here to bring condemnation; that's actually one of the reasons the Son of the Creator is coming. To relieve us of the burdens we carry around."

Mark laughed. "That's just it, man. I don't know why I've always felt this way, but I do know it goes against the usual order of things. I mean, look at you and Mary. You guys are the typical family. There's a man, woman and a baby on the way.

I'd give anything to have that…anything to be…" He stopped talking and held his head down.

I grabbed Mark's hand. "Mark, we all have desires to do things that aren't necessarily what the law allows. But that doesn't lessen the Creator's love for you. The Messiah will come and help us; He'll help you figure this out."

Mark looked up and smiled. "I've never told another soul about Charles. I've loved him the way people say I shouldn't, my entire life. I finally had to move out here and be away from him. People act as if I don't believe in the Creator, or that I don't believe in the Son, but I do. I'm just in a place of wondering why. If what I feel is wrong, then why do I feel this way?"

Joseph stood up and walked over to us. "I don't have the answer for that, Mark, but I know this. You're a good man. You've allowed Mary and I to stay here; even gave us your room. You have no idea the magnitude of what you have done, or who you have done it for." Joseph reached out and shook his hand.

Mark looked from Joseph's face to mine. "Why are you guys being so…nice?"

"What do you mean?" I asked and turned back toward the stove.

"Well, most people just tell me I'm on my way to the abyss. I've never met any believers that aren't hateful toward me, when they find out."

Joseph, who had walked back over to the table, almost shouted.

"And for that, we apologize, Mark. Anyone who condemns you for sin isn't acting like a child of the Creator. The enemy is the condemner of our brothers and sisters, and we are to show the Creator's love for you, even if we don't agree with you." Joseph sat down. "Look, I'm a dude. I find it repulsive that you would even consider liking another guy. But I'd be a hypocrite to treat you any differently than I would a liar, or someone that is doing something else that I believe is wrong."

Mark was so shocked by Joseph's behavior that he opened up even more. He'd been a believer all his life, but recently he said events persuaded him even more that the time of the Son was at hand. He explained.

"The prophecies speak of One who will come; a Child who will grow into a man to lead our people out of bondage. I believe the time is now."

"Why?" Joseph asked, obviously acting as if he had no knowledge of our baby.

Mark got up and walked around excitedly. "There are these scientists that have been secretly tracking the signs in the sky. The stars are aligning like they never have before. I heard a report from a cousin of mine, that they actually believe that the One will be born this year."

I choked on my drink, which sent Joseph flying out of his chair toward me. He patted me on the back until I could assure him that I was fine.

Mark looked over kindly. "Are you okay, Mary?"

I answered best I could. "Yeah," I said and coughed. "Just swallowed that down the wrong way."

Joseph sat back down, but kept his eyes on me. I nodded a few times so he would know I was fine, so he looked back over to Mark who continued.

"A buddy of mine from NASA said a few of their astronomers got canned last week for carrying on a secret study. None of them are known for being believers, but the government didn't like what they had apparently discovered. The guys all took off, and I think they're headed wherever they believe the Child is going to be born."

I leaned forward. "But how will they know? How will they know if it is the Son of the Creator?"

Mark smiled. "That's the coolest thing. All of this is based on prophecy and signs that have been logged by astronomers the decades. They compiled a lot of the data and put it in this machine that helped pinpoint the region. No one knows for sure where it is, but the NASA people say there will be an astronomical sign."

I thought about that for a moment. "So what will the three men do when they find the child?"

He shrugged. "Beats me. I just wonder what's going to happen if this is all true. It was just announced last week that Herod has turned his sights from men to children. One of his idiot advisors finally figured out the Creator was coming as a Child. I can't even imagine what his response to that is going to be. There's been no official word yet."

Someone called Mark's name from down the stairs and he stood to leave. He turned to Joseph.

"I wouldn't worry about it though. Herod isn't known for being the brightest light bulb. He'll probably start interrogating infants." He laughed as my heart jumped.

Mark went downstairs and Joseph got up and came over to my chair.

"I won't let anything hurt you or the baby, Mary. The Creator has been faithful, and I believe He will help me."

I grabbed onto Joseph. "I'm okay...I know everything will be okay."

He leaned up and sighed. "I'm going to go put the stuff

away out back. The truck is ready tomorrow, so we'll be on our way finally."

That was a relief to hear. "Thank the Creator," I said. "I was beginning to get used to all these city noises."

Joseph laughed. "By the time we get home, I'll have to sleep with the television on."

When he left, I went into the bedroom. I'd been so tired the past few days, and those familiar cramps kept hitting me off and on. I didn't want to worry Joseph, but as I lay thinking, another cramp hit me. Rest. I just needed to rest.

CHAPTER TWENTY-TWO

THE DESTINY OF MARY

BECAUSE Joseph had done so much work on the shop, Mark handed us a few hundred dollars. We were astounded, and Joseph tried to deny it, but Mark insisted. He said we had introduced him to compassion, and for once in his life, he'd felt the Creator's love through believers.

The truck ran great, and we were headed out by the afternoon. There were a few suburbs that surrounded the big city. The one we had to travel to, in order to register, was about a hundred miles. By nightfall, we should be able to find a place to stay, and the in the morning sign all the official paperwork and be done.

I had slept well the night before, so Joseph and I talked the majority of the ride. Ranches began to sprawl up along the drive, and we were surprised to find a place called Sheep Ranch Soul Food along the way. I wasn't sure what soul food was, but I was starving. We decided to stop and eat dinner there.

Even though we were only seventy miles or so from the city, this place was extremely removed from city life. There was an ease about it that reminded me of Joseph. It was calm, very relaxing and clean. The people in the diner were very hospitable, and for the first time since our journey began, I felt very comfortable.

The place was quiet, considering the amount of people that were here, and we immediately realized why as we ate. Our meal of friend chicken, mashed potatoes, cornbread and greens arrived in short order. The smells that emitted from my plate were salivating, and I dove in famished. Never in my life had I had food that was so filling and delicious. Joseph and I both were silent, and the only thing you could hear in the whole place was an old jukebox that still took quarters.

A nice lady came up and asked us if we wanted some sweet potato pie.

"What's that?" I asked.

She laughed. "Oh, honey, you sure aren't from around here, are ya? Why sweet potato pie is heaven on a plate."

I smiled. "What do you think, Joseph?" I turned and looked at him. "Do you think we could handle a little heaven on earth?"

He rolled his eyes at my obvious personal joke. "I think we could handle that," he answered and winked at me. I blushed.

Five minutes later we believed she hadn't lied. That pie was the fluffiest, lightest, sweetest and most savory thing I had ever eaten. I'd never be able to confess it to my mother, but sweet potato pie had become my new favorite dessert.

After dinner I went to the bathroom. I was so full and thankful. The baby had gotten so big, it was a challenge to maneuver out of the small stall, but I managed. As I was washing my hands, one of those familiar cramps hit me again. I'd gotten used to them over the past couple of days, but this one tightened, and I found myself gripping the side of the sink.

For a moment I thought it wouldn't end, but after thirty

seconds or so it did. I fixed my hair and walked back out to the dining room. Joseph was talking to a few people, and when I walked up, he looked concerned. One of the men was speaking.

"Yep, they said the government troops just made their way into the city."

"What's Herod up to now?" Another man asked.

"I don't know, but I've got a brother there who says they are all in the streets. It's like they're looking for somebody, but they're not saying who. So far, they haven't done much but scare a few folks."

Joseph squeezed my hand and then led me toward the door.

"Mary, we're going to reach our destination in a few hours. We'll register in the morning, and I think we should start back right away. I was talking to those guys, and there's another route home that will help us avoid the militia."

"But how long, Joseph? The baby is due in another week," I said concerned.

He opened the door and we walked out into the night. "I know, Mary, but this is what's best. I don't know what Herod's soldiers are doing, and I'm not going to risk exposing you and the baby. I feel it in my gut."

I nodded and got into the truck. Joseph went around, got in and handed me something.

"Surprise," he said elated. I looked down to see a food container.

"What's this?" I asked intrigued.

"A little bit of heaven on earth," he said, mimicking the accent of the woman from the diner.

"Oh, thank you," I said and leaned over to hug him. I was stopped short by a wave of pain.

"Ow," I said holding onto my stomach.

"What's wrong?" He asked and turned on the interior light.

The pain left within seconds. I shrugged. "I probably have gas," I admitted with a laugh.

"Are you sure?" He asked and turned the light back out.

"Yeah, I'm sure. Let's just get going. The faster we get there, the faster we can leave."

Thirty miles wasn't too much further, and we made it in about an hour. Within that one hour, I'd had four of those waves of pain, but I leaned against the door so Joseph wouldn't be alarmed.

I feigned sleep as long as I could, but the waves of pain escalated and got too uncomfortable. I heard myself make a strange noise, and Joseph flipped the overhead light on again.

"Mary, you alright?"

I was going to say yes, but another wave of pain hit me, and it was obvious I was not okay.

"Mary," he said, this time pulling over to the side of the road.

I shook my head. "I don't know, Joseph. I just don't feel very well."

He looked more than concerned. "What do you mean?"

I shifted in the seat, trying to get more comfortable, but it didn't work.

"Where are we?" I asked, noticing some small structures ahead.

"We just got into the town limits. There's not much here, but I'm trying to find a place to stay. Looks mostly like houses."

Another pain hit me like a wave, making me tense every part of my body. My stomach seemed to contort into this weird shape, and something in me clicked.

"Joseph," I whispered.

"Yeah," he said and took my hand.

"I think it's the baby."

He looked at me blankly. "The baby?"

I nodded. "I think it's time for me to have the baby."

Right as those words left my mouth, I felt a weird sensation in my lower abdomen. I felt like I had peed on myself.

"Oh...my..." I started to say, but a wave of pain hit me and it came out like a yell.

"Mary!" Joseph yelled and I squeezed his hand.

"It's time, Joseph. We need to find a hospital, or a doctor or something," I said beginning to panic.

Joseph started the truck and gunned the engine. As we went past structures, I could see he was right. There was nothing out here. The structures I saw looked like shabby little homes. We went fast, racing down the long stretch of highway, and up ahead looked like a bigger building just off the road. It had to be an inn or a bed and breakfast.

The truck stopped sharply into park, and with the engine running Joseph hopped out and ran in. He came out a minute later with his hands on his head. Opening the driver's side door, he hopped in and backed out of the driveway.

"What are you doing?" I asked agitated.

"There's no room there, Mary," he answered solemnly.

"No room?" I yelled. "Did you tell them I was having a baby?" I grabbed onto my knees and moaned.

"I told them, but the guy wouldn't even let me explain. The place was packed; some people were even sleeping on the floor in the living room."

The pain mounted and I didn't even care anymore. All I knew was the baby was coming, and there wasn't anything I could do about it. I tried to remain calm, but I'd never done this before. I had no idea what to expect, or what to do.

Joseph pulled off onto a dirt road. I realized he was in someone's front yard, but I didn't care. He hopped out and came back a minute later.

"That guy's got no room either, but he said there's a feed shed outback that we can use."

"A feed shed?" I asked with my teeth clinched. "But what about the baby? What about a doctor?"

"There's nothing else, Mary," Joseph answered.

At that point I didn't care. I cried as we made it over some bumps and then the truck stopped.

"I've got to open the gate," he explained.

A few moments later he was back, and the ride continued. I didn't know where this feed shed was, but I knew I couldn't stay in the truck like this any longer. Resisting the urge to push, I reached out and grabbed the dashboard. I couldn't tell what kind of noise I made, but the look on Joseph's face when I turned to him was determined.

"Hold on, Mary," he said as the truck came to a stop.

"Joseph!" I screamed, suddenly overwhelmed with pain. Everywhere felt like it was in pain, and my stomach was as hard as a rock. I felt a sensation of warmth spread across the lower half of my body and I needed to push.

Joseph got out, ran around the truck and opened the door. Effortlessly he picked me up and we made our way into the feed shed. The headlights from the truck shone through the door, as he laid me down on the ground. It smelled like fresh hay, and I grabbed onto it as another pain hit me.

Thunder crashed outside, and the wind picked up and raced through the small shed. Joseph helped me take off my jacket, and then slipped off my shoes and jeans. I was in so much pain I cried, saying my mother's name over and over again.

Everything was hot and I wanted to squeeze my legs together to make the pain stop, but then an urge to push would hit me. I could hear Joseph yell at me to push, and I'd bear down with all my might and push.

It seemed to go on for hours, if not days. One wave of pain met into another, and I thought it would never end. All of a sudden it felt like I'd sat on a hot poker and one push later... He was there.

I'd seen a movie once about the birth of a baby. This was nothing like it. Joseph held our newborn son in his hands, and I could see tears glistening down Joseph's face. He laid him on my stomach, and I touched our son. The Creator in the flesh had come.

He looked at me as if He already knew me. My small wee son let out a sweet cry, as if singing with a yawn. He made no other sound, but His eyes remained locked on mine. It was as if I was seeing the past, present and future all at once. There would never be another moment like this on this earth. It was everything.

"There's no umbilical cord," Joseph said quietly. "There's nothing else....inside...I mean, I guess..." His voice trailed off obviously confounded.

I looked down at my son's tiny, perfect body, and he had no belly button. I knew then that I had just been a vessel for the most glorious birth there would ever be. He was not part of me, but He was here for me. This Child was born to save us.

I cried, and Joseph startled me by jumping up and running to the truck. He was back in a moment. He placed a simple, familiar blanket on the baby.

"How did you get that?" I asked, tucking it around the baby.

"I went back and got it. The lady remembered you and gave it to me for ten dollars. She said you were meant to have it." Joseph looked down at the baby. "I guess she was right."

I realized we had nothing else for the Creator's Son. Everything we'd bought Him was at home, and we hadn't planned on what to do, in the event that we had Him on the road.

Joseph smoothed my hair. "Are you okay?"

"Yeah," I responded. "I am now."

Thunder and lightning rippled throughout the sky. At one point, it was so bright, it was as if a giant flashlight beam was directed at us, but no rain ever fell. The night went on in such a fashion, and I believed it had to have been the heavenly host rejoicing over the birth of the Son.

I wanted to get cleaned up best I could, so Joseph took the baby in his arms. I was so weak after the birth that I couldn't get around unsupported, so Joseph scooted over a manger that had been discarded. He put fresh hay in it, and lay our son, who was sleeping, down gently.

With bottled water from the truck and a trough that was outside, Joseph helped me clean up and get a fresh change of clothing on. Within thirty minutes I was feeling much better, and he propped up some things from the truck to make me more comfortable.

Just when we got done, a noise outside startled us. Joseph had taken the gun out and laid it beside me. He reached for it and walked toward the door. Silhouetted by the truck head-lights, I saw figures approaching us.

I reached over and grabbed Jesus out of the manger, hugging

Him to me protectively. Joseph stood positioned in front of me, and I saw him slowly raise the gun. He lowered it a moment later, and I was shocked that he moved aside.

A couple of men were coming in the door. They were dressed in rancher's gear, and one of them was very old. He came and knelt in front of me, tears streaming down his face into his beard.

"He is here," he said in a gruff voice. "The Messiah is here." With that, he fell to his knees in front of me and wept. I realized that he had come to worship our Creator in flesh. Somehow they knew.

The men behind him all followed his example, and fresh tears fell from my eyes at their wonderment. The baby cooed, so I held Him around for others to see Him better. The man raised his head at the sound of the baby and smiled.

"Oh, Lord. What blessed thing you have done," he said.

Just then a vehicle pulled up. Joseph was immediately at the door, shielding his eyes from the additional set of headlights.

It was a huge vehicle. Not the size of one I had ever seen before. Three figures walked our way, and once again they knelt. The one closest to the door got up and came to sit by me. He looked down at Jesus.

"Behold, the star has led us to find our Savior," He said. "We bring him gifts, fit for a king...the King of all kings." He then reached out and set something by me. "Gold for my King," he said and bowed down.

The next man came, knelt and extended something. "The gift of frankincense; an offering we give to our Priest."

The third man came, also knelt and spoke. "We give Him Myrrh, to symbolize the sacrifice of becoming flesh to dwell among us."

Their words washed over me with warmth. The reverence in this moment in a feed shed, highlighted by the headlights of a Ford truck...were priceless.

EPILOGUE

THE three men and the ranchers stayed for a week. We all worshiped our newborn King, and the time went so quickly. I rested most of the time, and after I'd slept, I'd awake to more presents or gifts.

The ranchers had left and come back with more food, and the astronomers had brought books and things that they thought would help in the days to come. Using short wave radios, they taught us how to remain undetected by the government.

We had heard reports that more and more militia were showing up all over the country. Herod hadn't made a move yet, so no one knew exactly what he was doing, or when he was going to do it.

As the days went by, I felt stronger and stronger. The ranchers brought back a few items from town for the baby, and I believed we'd be able to travel home with Him safely. One of them even brought us back the coolest car seat. He said the Creator had impressed upon him to buy it weeks ago, though he wasn't married and had no children. He obeyed, and upon the birth of my son, was thankful for his obedience.

We went to bed that night warm and full, and I figured we'd start for home in a couple more days. We didn't risk calling my parents. The astronomers said it wouldn't be safe, considering that Herod had learned the truth of the Creator's child like entrance on earth. So we decided to head back home the next day without notifying anyone that the Son had been born.

The fire crackled as another rancher threw a log on the fire. I had just got done feeding Jesus, when Joseph jumped up out of his sleep with a terrified look on his face.

"What is it?" I asked alarmed at the amount of perspiration that dripped from his forehead.

"We've got to go," he said and jumped up.

"What do you mean?" I asked looking around. "I thought we were leaving in a day or two."

"Mary," he said kneeling down next to me. "Listen to me. Get all of Jesus' things together and put him in the car seat. We have to go now."

He left and I saw him speaking to a few of the men. They were all shaking their heads, and the tension of the moment rose. People began to scatter, and Joseph helped me gather the last of the baby's things.

It wasn't until he had hooked the car seat into the front of the truck, that he turned to me and spoke.

"An angel spoke to me again, Mary."

I gasped. "What?"

Joseph nodded. "You know how Herod is sending militia throughout the area?"

"Yeah," I said worried.

"The angel said they want to harm the baby. I've got to get you and Jesus out of here, but we can't go home."

Tears formed in my eyes. "We can't go home?"

He opened the passenger side of the truck and helped me in. Joseph leaned in and kissed me on the cheek and shut the door.

I couldn't understand this. What had happened? How

would Herod even know which baby was Jesus? No one was even around.

Joseph peeled out of the drive and headed toward the highway.

"But what about the census? Won't we get in trouble if you don't register?"

"One of the ranchers and his wife are going to take care of it for us. The agency only asked for I.D. and a signature. I gave him my driver's license and yours. After we get settled some place, I'll contact him to get them back. In the meantime, the angel told me a safe place for us to go."

I wiped the tears from my face and looked down at Jesus. "And you're sure they won't find us?" I asked and smoothed His little hand.

"They won't," Joseph answered decidedly. "The Creator wouldn't have warned me and told me where to go for no reason. Everything will be okay, Mary."

"What are my parents going to think?" I asked looking out the window.

"They'll know we're okay...He'll let them know."

The lights on the highway beamed bright as we headed south. I wasn't sure where we were going, but as I looked over at my husband, I knew he would keep us safe. The Child that sat in the car seat between us was all that mattered.

I closed my eyes and looked skyward. The Creator had been with me along this journey, and provided in ways that I couldn't explain. I had to believe now that my destiny had just begun. The Destiny of Mary...mother of Jesus.